ELIZABETH VON ARNIM

(1866—1941) was born Mary Annette Beauchamp in Sydney, Australia, and brought up in England. Travelling in Italy with her father in 1889, she met her first husband, Count Henning August von Arnim-Schlagenthin, a grandson of Prince Augustus of Prussia. They were married in London the following year and lived in Berlin. After five years of marriage the von Arnims moved to their family estate, Nassenheide, in Pomerania: Elizabeth's experience and deep love of Nassenheide were to be wittily encapsulated in her first and most famous novel, *Elizabeth and Her German Garden*, published anonymously in 1898. The twenty-one books she then went on to write were signed "By the author of Elizabeth and Her German Garden", and later simply "By Elizabeth".

Elizabeth von Arnim gave birth to four daughters and a son, whose tutors at Nassenheide included E. M. Forster and Hugh Walpole. Her idyllic Prussian days were, however, to be abruptly ended when, in 1908, debt forced the von Arnims to sell the estate. They moved to England, and in 1910 Count von Arnim died. Buying a site in Switzerland, Elizabeth built the Chateau Soleil where she worked on her books and entertained such friends as H. G. Wells (with whom she had an affair), Katherine Mansfield (her cousin), John Middleton Murry and Frank Swinnerton. On the outbreak of war she managed to escape to England, though was unable to rescue her daughter Felicitas, who died in Germany. In 1916 Elizabeth von Arnim married Francis, second Earl Russell, brother of Bertrand Russell, whom she had met three years previously. This proved to be a disastrous union: in the first year of marriage Elizabeth ran away to America, and in 1919 the couple finally separated.

A greatly admired literary figure of her time, described by Alice Meynell as "one of the three finest wits of her day", Elizabeth spent her later years in Switzerland, London, and the French Riviera where she wrote her autobiography, *All the Dogs of My Life* (1936). On the outbreak of the Second World War she moved to America, where she died two years later at the age of seventy-five.

Of her novels Virago publish *Vera, Fraulein Schmidt and Mr Anstruther* and *Elizabeth and Her German Garden. The Enchanted April* will be published in 1986.

VIRAGO
MODERN
CLASSIC

NUMBER
173

ELIZABETH AND HER GERMAN GARDEN

ELIZABETH VON ARNIM

With a New Introduction by
Elizabeth Jane Howard

Virago

Published by VIRAGO PRESS Limited 1985
41 William IV Street, London WC2N 4DB

First published in Great Britain by Macmillan and Co. Ltd 1898

Virago edition offset from Macmillan 1929 edition

Copyright Elizabeth von Arnim 1898

Introduction copyright © Elizabeth Jane Howard 1985

British Library Cataloguing in Publication Data

von Arnim, Elizabeth
  Elizabeth and her German garden
  I. Title
  823[F]   PR9619.3.V/

ISBN 0-86068-423-7

Printed in Great Britain by Cox and
Wyman of Reading, Berkshire

INTRODUCTION

In 1889 Henry Beauchamp took his youngest daughter May
to Italy. He expected his wife to join them in a week or so
when he would be able to abandon the exigencies of
chaperoning a young girl and—leaving the women to their
own devices—get down to some really serious sightseeing on
his own—a practice to which he had become increasingly
addicted since he had come from Australia and settled in
Europe. Mary Annette—the family called her May—had
acquitted herself well at school where she won a prize for
History and also at the Royal College of Music where she had
won a prize for organ playing. She was twenty-three, and
had earlier been described by her father, who had only lately
begun to appreciate her, as "bright, industrious and good".

Mr Beauchamp's sightseeing itinerary—even with a young
and giddy daughter addicted to cake shops—was
formidable. They visited Milan, Genoa, Pisa and finally
Rome, looking at everything that was to be seen and only sat
down when they took Italian lessons or paid calls upon the
people to whom they had introductions. May's musical
ability must have been out of the ordinary as one of the
introductions was given her by Sir George Groves of the
Royal College to a famous Roman musician in whose house,
after calling, they spent the entire evening. "Just as we were

going to bed 'Il Conte' appeared dressed up to the eyes on his way to a ball at the Quirinal Palace and staid over an hour." (Mr Beauchamp's Journal)

"Il Conte" was the German Graf Henning August von Arnim-Schlagenthin who was travelling to get over the death of his wife and child who had died the previous year. He was immediately attracted to May, and when, a month after their meeting he heard her playing Bach at organ recitals in the American Church in Rome, he was determined to marry her. There followed a brief, but intensely romantic courtship as von Arnim pursued the Beauchamps in Italy, in Switzerland and Germany, eventually persuading the family to take rooms in Bayreuth. Many years later Elizabeth was to write to Hugh Walpole, "my first courted me in Bayreuth and there's not a tree within five miles that I haven't been kissed under".

By the end of July their engagement was official: von Arnim did not want to wait long for the marriage, but he said that it was absolutely necessary for May to learn German, in order to manage the servants. She therefore spent three months in Dresden with her mother, having a lesson every day. The marriage took place the following February in London, and after a honeymoon in Paris, they settled to upper-class German life in Berlin, which for May (who at this point seems to have been translated into Elizabeth) was a period of stultifying dullness. She was homesick for England and her family: she somewhat mutinously bore three daughters in as many years (von Arnim was desperate for a son); she paid and received calls, went to and gave parties, received instruction in dress and etiquette—and languished.

Then, in 1896, she accompanied her husband on one of his regular visits to his enormous Pomeranian estate, Nassenheide, ninety miles north of Berlin. The estate was centred upon a large seventeenth-century schloss that had once been a convent and had been unoccupied for the previous twenty-five years. It was surrounded by a vast,

INTRODUCTION

rambling and derelict garden. The moment that she saw it,
Elizabeth knew that she wanted to live there. Here was
freedom and peace; a natural isolation from the
soul-destroying social life of Berlin—a wilderness of beauty
to be ordered and enjoyed. In spite of some difficulty in
persuading von Arnim (who had spent practically all his life
in cities, was fifteen years older than she and a Prussian to
boot), she got his partial agreement to their living there—at
least for the summer months.

Elizabeth and Her German Garden was published two
years later, and opens with her account of the first blissful
weeks from April to June when she was alone there,
supposedly superintending the painting and papering of the
house, but in fact spending every waking moment in the wild
garden, with its bird cherries, lilacs, wild flowers and four
great clumps of pale silvery-pink paeonies. Her meals of
salad and bread and tea—with the occasional tiny pigeon to
save her from starvation—were brought to her in the garden
on trays, and she spent her reluctant nights alone in the old
house with her door locked and a dinner bell by her as a
weapon against fear.

This first book, published anonymously, was an instant
success, reprinting eleven times in the first year, and with
twenty-one editions printed by May 1899. It received a good
press on the whole, although one reviewer grumbled that
"even the amateur gardener will be disappointed, for he will
find therein no tips as to the best methods of grafting apples,
or of destroying vermin . . ." and the *Spectator*, in the person
of Quiller-Couch, complained that he found her "not only
selfish, but quite inhumanly so and her mind . . . of that
order which finds a smart self-satisfaction in proclaiming
how thoroughly it is dominated by self." The *Derby Mercury*
felt sure that the anonymous author was a gentleman,
"betraying his sex by more than one sign" but on the whole
The Times—in spite of its rather patronising attitude—
conveys the most general contemporary response to the

book.

The anonymous author of *Elizabeth and Her German Garden*
has written a very bright little book—genial, humorous, perhaps
a little fantastic and wayward here and there, but full of bright
glimpses of nature and sprightly criticisms of life. Elizabeth is the
English wife of a German husband, who finds and makes for
herself a delightful retreat from the banalities of life in a German
provincial town by occupying and beautifying a deserted
convent, the property of her husband, in one of the Baltic
provinces. Her gardening experiences are somewhat primitive
and unsophisticated, but this is, no doubt, only a harmless
literary artifice, for the charm of the book lies not in its
horticultural record, but in its personal atmosphere, its
individuality of sentiment, its healthy sympathy with nature and
outdoor life,its shrewd but kindly appreciations of character and
social circumstance. There is a pleasant sub-acid flavour in some
of Elizabeth's pages which show that she could do better if she
chose; but she is seldom ungenerous except in the remarks about
nurses and their ways which she puts into the mouth of her
husband, and is never dull.

The book—described rather loosely as a novel—*is* an
extraordinary piece of work. It has an idyllic quality;
Elizabeth's joy and excitement about transforming a
wilderness into a garden is seconded only by her desire
simply to revel in the place—to become part of a great and
continuing pastoral romance—of the seasons, the times of
the day, of the weather, of all the amazing machinery of
nature that provided such infinite variation. Her enthusiasm
is matched by her self-confessed ignorance: she buys *ten
pounds* of ipomaea seed – sows it in eleven beds and "round
nearly every tree, and waited in great agitation for the
promised paradise to appear. It did not, and I learned my
first lesson." It did not matter, she had the wild flowers—the
old lawns that had become meadows filled with "every pretty
sort of weed". The opening of the book contains the ecstasy
of a release that every woman who has experienced marriage
and motherhood will recognise and many will envy: the
opportunity to be alone, to have space and privacy with no

demands made upon her, to eat and sleep and read when she pleased, to have silence and solitude and the time to be with herself—all things that no doubt people like Quiller-Couch would regard as infra dig, selfish, unbecoming and unnecessary for a woman. But a singular aspect of this book is the author's determination to be something more than a good German wife and mother, and it is this quality, set against the more traditionally romantic hymn to nature that gives the work its unique flavour.

In the midst of the first few weeks of this solitary paradise, her husband arrives to rebuke her for not having written. She says that she has been too happy to think of writing. This, unsurprisingly, does not reassure him—he thinks it extraordinary that she should be happy in his absence and the absence of the children. She shows him her beloved lilacs and he remarks that they badly need pruning, she offers him her salad and toast supper "but nothing appeased the Man of Wrath, and he said he would go straight back to the neglected family". Henceforward, in her book, he is known as the Man of Wrath, and her relationship with him (she was in conflict with his private as well as his formal demands) adds an original dimension to the book. There seems to be no doubt but that he was devoted to her—found her fascinating and rewarding company, and was only occasionally put out by her eccentricities—her spending her pin money on artificial manure, for instance. Her portrait of the Man of Wrath is affectionately satirical—she teases him, but he comes well out of it—she feeds the liberal, eccentric aspect of his nature, but she has the rest of him to contend with, and this she does throughout with a most daring tact.*

Her children, called throughout the April, May and June baby respectively, make welcome appearances. Here is

*It is interesting to note that another von Arnim, a cousin of the Man of Wrath, had seventy-nine years earlier married Bettina Brentano—a militant romantic, gifted and eccentric, and much of Elizabeth's behaviour and personality is reminiscent of her.

INTRODUCTION

Elizabeth about the April baby and a governess.

> . . . Miss Jones cast down her eyes. She is always perpetually scenting a scene, and is always ready to bring whole batteries of discretion and tact and good taste to bear on us . . . I would take my courage in both hands and ask her to go . . . but unfortunately the April baby adores her and is sure that never was anyone so beautiful before. She comes every day with fresh accounts of the splendours of her wardrobe, and feeling descriptions of her umbrellas and hats. In common with most governesses she has a little dark down on her upper lip, and the April baby appeared one day at dinner with her own decorated in faithful imitation, having achieved it after much struggling with the aid of a lead pencil and much love. Miss Jones put her in a corner for impertinence. I wonder why governesses are so unpleasant? The Man of Wrath says it is because they are not married. I would add that the strain of continually having to set an example must surely be very great. It is much easier, and often more pleasant, to be a warning than an example . . .

The garden is her escape from domestic duties; indeed, with the exception of the "white and yellow library", the house is hardly described at all. It is the garden that is her element—the place where she can breathe and live, meditate, dream, plan and above all, read. Elizabeth was a voracious reader. Books accompanied her everywhere, and it would seem that during those early years at Nassenheide she was, perhaps unconsciously, preparing herself for her subsequent career as a writer (by the end of her life she had published twenty-two books). But even her dauntless spirit was sometimes circumscribed by the rules of her society.

> I wish with all my heart I were a man, for of course the first thing I should do would be to buy a spade and go and garden, and then I should have the delight of doing everything for my flowers with my own hands, and need not waste time explaining what I want done to somebody else. It is dull work giving orders and trying to describe the bright visions of one's brain to a person who has no visions and no brain, and who thinks a yellow bed should be calceolarias edged with blue.

And again . . .

In the first ecstasy of having a garden all my own, and in my burning impatience to make the waste places blossom like a rose, I did one warm Sunday in last year's April during the servants' dinner hour, double secure from the gardener by the day and the dinner, slink out with a spade and a rake and feverishly dig a little piece of ground and break it up and sow surreptitious ipomæa and run back very hot and guilty into the house and get into a chair and behind a book and look languid just in time to save my reputation. And why not? It is not graceful, and it makes one hot; but it is a blessed sort of work, and if Eve had had a spade in Paradise and known what to do with it, we should not have had all that sad business with the apple.

When we consider all the skilled and fulfilled women gardeners who have flourished in this century, the frustration for poor Elizabeth is poignant.

Elizabeth was ahead of her time in that she envisaged an English garden, and what she meant by that was *not* the vast elaborate geometry of bedding plants en parterre, but rather a merging of cultivated plants with the wild—a blending of garden to park—an apparent carelessness that was none the less artful. E. M. Forster, who stayed at Nassenheide in 1904 as tutor to her children, in complaining about the garden unconsciously describes it rather well:

I couldn't find it. The house appeared to be surrounded by paddock and shrubberies. Later on, some flowers—mostly pansies—came into bloom. Also rose-trees in the little whirligig of laid-out beds. But there was nothing of a show—only the lilacs effected that, and the white flowering faulbaum by which the dykes were edged. Nor did Elizabeth take any interest in flowers. The garden merged in the "park" which was sylvan in tendency and consisted of small copses ... There was also a field in the park, over whose long grass, at the end of July, a canopy of butterflies kept waving.

And Hugh Walpole, also a tutor remarked in 1907: "the garden is becoming beautiful in a wild rather uncouth kind of way, but it is a garden of trees rather than flowers". These two may have been highly educated in some respects, but their expectations of a garden were fashionably common-place compared to Elizabeth's.

She went on to write some very good novels, but *Elizabeth and Her German Garden*, its more rhapsodic passages nicely balanced by her acute and sometimes very funny perceptions about her family and friends, has a freshness, a freakish charm, an irrepressible energy that springs straight from the very source of her personality. It has also the seeds of an interesting and original exposition of the conflict between liberty and oppression that in her day it was taken for granted was the lot of women—a theme that was to occupy her in her writing life for many years to come.

Elizabeth Jane Howard, London, 1984

ELIZABETH AND HER GERMAN GARDEN

May 7th.—I love my garden. I am writing in it now in the late afternoon loveliness, much interrupted by the mosquitoes and the temptation to look at all the glories of the new green leaves washed half an hour ago in a cold shower. Two owls are perched near me, and are carrying on a long conversation that I enjoy as much as any warbling of nightingales. The gentleman owl says , and she answers from her tree a little way off, , beautifully assenting to and completing her lord's remark, as becomes a properly constructed German she-owl. They say the same thing over and over again so emphatically that

I think it must be something nasty about me ; but I shall not let myself be frightened away by the sarcasm of owls.

This is less a garden than a wilderness. No one has lived in the house, much less in the garden, for twenty-five years, and it is such a pretty old place that the people who might have lived here and did not, deliberately preferring the horrors of a flat in a town, must have belonged to that vast number of eyeless and earless persons of whom the world seems chiefly composed. Noseless too, though it does not sound pretty ; but the greater part of my spring happiness is due to the scent of the wet earth and young leaves.

I am always happy (out of doors be it understood, for indoors there are servants and furniture), but in quite different ways, and my spring happiness bears no resemblance to my summer or autumn happiness, though it is not more intense, and there were days last winter when I danced for sheer joy out in my frost-bound garden in spite of my years and children. But I

did it behind a bush, having a due regard
for the decencies.

There are so many bird-cherries round me,
great trees with branches sweeping the grass,
and they are so wreathed just now with
white blossoms and tenderest green that
the garden looks like a wedding. I never
saw such masses of them; they seem to fill
the place. Even across a little stream that
bounds the garden on the east, and right in
the middle of the cornfield beyond, there is
an immense one, a picture of grace and glory
against the cold blue of the spring sky.

My garden is surrounded by cornfields and
meadows, and beyond are great stretches of
sandy heath and pine forests, and where the
forests leave off the bare heath begins again;
but the forests are beautiful in their lofty,
pink-stemmed vastness, far overhead the
crowns of softest gray-green, and underfoot
a bright green whortleberry carpet, and
everywhere the breathless silence ; and the
bare heaths are beautiful too, for one can
see across them into eternity almost, and to
go out on to them with one's face towards

the setting sun is like going into the very presence of God.

In the middle of this plain is the oasis of bird-cherries and greenery where I spend my happy days, and in the middle of the oasis is the gray stone house with many gables where I pass my reluctant nights. The house is very old, and has been added to at various times. It was a convent before the Thirty Years' War, and the vaulted chapel, with its brick floor worn by pious peasant knees, is now used as a hall. Gustavus Adolphus and his Swedes passed through more than once, as is duly recorded in archives still preserved, for we are on what was then the high-road between Sweden and Branden- burg the unfortunate. The Lion of the North was no doubt an estimable person and acted wholly up to his convictions, but he must have sadly upset the peaceful nuns, who were not without convictions of their own, sending them out on to the wide, empty plain to piteously seek some life to replace the life of silence here.

From nearly all the windows of the house

I can look out across the plain, with no
obstacle in the shape of a hill, right away to
a blue line of distant forest, and on the west
side uninterruptedly to the setting sun—
nothing but a green, rolling plain, with a
sharp edge against the sunset.   I love those
west windows better than any others, and
have chosen my bedroom on that side of
the house so that even times of hair-brushing
may not be entirely lost, and the young
woman who attends to such matters has
been taught to fulfil her duties about a
mistress recumbent in an easy-chair before
an open window, and to not profane with
chatter that sweet and solemn time.   This
girl is grieved at my habit of living almost
in the garden, and all her ideas as to the sort
of life a respectable German lady should lead
have got into a sad muddle since she came to
me.   The people round about are persuaded
that I am, to put it as kindly as possible,
exceedingly eccentric, for the news has
travelled that I spend the day out of doors
with a book, and that no mortal eye has ever
yet seen me sew or cook.   But why cook

when you can get some one to cook for you? And as for sewing, the maids will hem the sheets better and quicker than I could, and all forms of needlework of the fancy order are inventions of the evil one for keeping the foolish from applying their hearts to wisdom.

We had been married five years before it struck us that we might as well make use of this place by coming down and living in it. Those five years were spent in a flat in a town, and during their whole interminable length I was perfectly miserable and perfectly healthy, which disposes of the ugly notion that has at times disturbed me that my happiness here is less due to the garden than to a good digestion. And while we were wasting our lives there, here was this dear place with dandelions up to the very door, all the paths grass-grown and completely effaced, in winter so lonely, with nobody but the north wind taking the least notice of it, and in May—in all those five lovely Mays—no one to look at the wonderful bird-cherries and still more wonderful masses of lilacs, everything glowing and blowing, the virginia creeper madder every year until at last, in October, the very roof was wreathed with blood-red tresses, the owls and the squirrels and all the blessed little birds reigning supreme, and not a living creature ever entering the empty house except the snakes, which got into the habit during those silent years of wriggling up the south wall into the rooms on that side whenever the old housekeeper opened the windows. All that was here—peace, and happiness, and a reasonable life, and yet it never struck me to come and live in it. Looking back I am astonished, and can in no way account for the tardiness of my discovery that here, in this far-away corner, was my kingdom of heaven. Indeed, so little did it enter my head to even use the place in summer, that I submitted to weeks of seaside life with all its horrors every year ; until at last, in the early spring of last year, having come down for the opening of the village school, and wandering out afterwards into the bare and desolate garden, I don't know what smell of wet earth or rotting leaves brought back my childhood with a rush and all the happy days I had spent in a garden. Shall I ever forget that day? It was the beginning of my real life, my coming of age as it were, and entering into my kingdom. Early March, gray, quiet skies, and brown, quiet earth; leafless and sad and lonely enough out there in the damp and silence, yet there I stood feeling the same rapture of pure delight in the first breath of spring that I used to as a child, and the five wasted years fell from me like a cloak, and the world was full of hope, and I vowed myself then and there to nature and have been happy ever since.

My other half being indulgent, and with some faint thought perhaps that it might be as well to look after the place, consented to live in it at any rate for a time; whereupon followed six specially blissful weeks from the end of April into June, during which I was here alone, supposed to be superintending the painting and papering, but as a matter of fact only going into the house when the workmen had gone out of it.

How happy I was! I don't remember any time quite so perfect since the days when I was too little to do lessons and was turned out with sugar on my eleven o'clock bread and butter on to a lawn closely strewn with dandelions and daisies. The sugar on the bread and butter has lost its charm, but I love the dandelions and daisies even more passionately now than then, and never would endure to see them all mown away if I were not certain that in a day or two they would be pushing up their little faces again as jauntily as ever. During those six weeks I lived in a world of dandelions and delights. The dandelions carpeted the three lawns— they used to be lawns, but have long since blossomed out into meadows filled with every sort of pretty weed—and under and among the groups of leafless oaks and beeches were blue hepaticas, white anemones, violets, and celandines in sheets. The celandines in particular delighted me with their clean, happy brightness, so beautifully trim and newly varnished, as though they too had had the painters at work on them. Then, when the anemones went, came a few stray periwinkles and Solomon's Seal, and all the bird-cherries blossomed in a burst. And then, before I had a little got used to the joy of their flowers against the sky, came the lilacs—masses and masses of them, in clumps on the grass, with other shrubs and trees by the side of walks, and one great continuous bank of them half a mile long right past the west front of the house, away down as far as one could see, shining glorious against a background of firs. When that time came, and when, before it was over, the acacias all blossomed too, and four great clumps of pale, silvery-pink peonies flowered under the south windows, I felt so absolutely happy, and blest, and thankful, and grateful, that I really cannot describe it. My days seemed to melt away in a dream of pink and purple peace.

There were only the old housekeeper and her handmaiden in the house, so that on the plea of not giving too much trouble I could indulge what my other half calls my *fantaisie déréglée* as regards meals—that is to say, meals so simple that they could be brought out to the lilacs on a tray ; and I lived, I remember, on salad and bread and tea the whole time, sometimes a very tiny pigeon appearing at lunch to save me, as the old lady thought, from starvation. Who but a woman could have stood salad for six weeks, even salad sanctified by the presence and scent of the most gorgeous lilac masses ? I did, and grew in grace every day, though I have never liked it since. How often now, oppressed by the necessity of assisting at three dining-room meals daily, two of which are conducted by the functionaries held indispensable to a proper maintenance of the family dignity, and all of which are pervaded by joints of meat, how often do I think of my salad days, forty in number, and of the blessedness of being alone as I was then alone !

And then the evenings, when the workmen had all gone and the house was left to emptiness and echoes, and the old housekeeper had gathered up her rheumatic limbs into her bed, and my little room in quite another part of the house had been set ready, how reluctantly I used to leave the friendly frogs and owls, and with my heart somewhere down in my shoes lock the door to the garden behind me, and pass through the long series of echoing south rooms full of shadows and ladders and ghostly pails of painters' mess, and humming a tune to make myself believe I liked it, go rather slowly across the brick-floored hall, up the creaking stairs, down the long whitewashed passage, and with a final rush of panic whisk into my room and double lock and bolt the door !

There were no bells in the house, and I used to take a great dinner-bell to bed with me so that at least I might be able to make a noise if frightened in the night, though what good it would have been I don't know, as there was no one to hear. The housemaid slept in another little cell opening out of mine, and we two were the only living creatures in the great empty west wing. She evidently did not believe in ghosts, for

I could hear how she fell asleep immediately after getting into bed ; nor do I believe in them, " *mais je les redoute,*" as a French lady said, who from her books appears to have been strong-minded.

The dinner-bell was a great solace ; it was never rung, but it comforted me to see it on the chair beside my bed, as my nights were anything but placid, it was all so strange, and there were such queer creakings and other noises. I used to lie awake for hours, startled out of a light sleep by the cracking of some board, and listen to the indifferent snores of the girl in the next room. In the morning, of course, I was as brave as a lion and much amused at the cold perspirations of the night before ; but even the nights seem to me now to have been delightful, and myself like those historic boys who heard a voice in every wind and snatched a fearful joy. I would gladly shiver through them all over again for the sake of the beautiful purity of the house, empty of servants and upholstery.

How pretty the bedrooms looked with

nothing in them but their cheerful new papers! Sometimes I would go into those that were finished and build all sorts of castles in the air about their future and their past. Would the nuns who had lived in them know their little whitewashed cells again, all gay with delicate flower papers and clean white paint? And how astonished they would be to see cell No. 14 turned into a bathroom, with a bath big enough to ensure a cleanliness of body equal to their purity of soul! They would look upon it as a snare of the tempter; and I know that in my own case I only began to be shocked at the blackness of my nails the day that I began to lose the first whiteness of my soul by falling in love at fifteen with the parish organist, or rather with the glimpse of surplice and Roman nose and fiery moustache which was all I ever saw of him, and which I loved to distraction for at least six months; at the end of which time, going out with my governess one day, I passed him in the street, and discovered that his unofficial garb was a frock-coat combined with a turn-down collar and a "bowler" hat, and never loved him any more.

The first part of that time of blessedness was the most perfect, for I had not a thought of anything but the peace and beauty all round me. Then he appeared suddenly who has a right to appear when and how he will and rebuked me for never having written, and when I told him that I had been literally too happy to think of writing he seemed to take it as a reflection on himself that I could be happy alone. I took him round the garden along the new paths I had had made, and showed him the acacia and lilac glories, and he said that it was the purest selfishness to enjoy myself when neither he nor the offspring were with me, and that the lilacs wanted thoroughly pruning. I tried to appease him by offering him the whole of my salad and toast supper which stood ready at the foot of the little verandah steps when we came back, but nothing appeased that Man of Wrath, and he said he would go straight back to the neglected family. So he went; and the remainder of the precious time was disturbed by twinges of conscience (to which I am much subject) whenever I found myself wanting to jump for joy. I went to look at the painters every time my feet were for taking me to look at the garden; I trotted diligently up and down the passages; I criticised and suggested and commanded more in one day than I had done in all the rest of the time; I wrote regularly and sent my love; but I could not manage to fret and yearn. What are you to do if your conscience is clear and your liver in order and the sun is shining?

May 10*th*.—I knew nothing whatever last year about gardening and this year know very little more, but I have dawnings of what may be done, and have at least made one great stride—from ipomæa to tea-roses.

The garden was an absolute wilderness. It is all round the house, but the principal part is on the south side and has evidently always been so. The south front is one-storied, a long series of rooms opening one into the other, and the walls are covered with

virginia creeper.   There is a little verandah
in the middle, leading by a flight of rickety
wooden steps down into what seems to have
been the only spot in the whole place that
was ever cared for.   This is a semicircle cut
into the lawn and edged with privet, and
in this semicircle are eleven beds of different
sizes bordered with box and arranged round
a sun-dial, and the sun-dial is very venerable and moss-grown, and greatly beloved by
me.   These beds were the only sign of any
attempt at gardening to be seen (except a
solitary crocus that came up all by itself each
spring in the grass, not because it wanted
to, but because it could not help it), and
these I had sown with ipomæa, the whole
eleven, having found a German gardening
book, according to which ipomæa in vast
quantities was the one thing needful to
turn the most hideous desert into a paradise.
Nothing else in that book was recommended
with anything like the same warmth, and
being entirely ignorant of the quantity of
seed necessary, I bought ten pounds of it
and had it sown not only in the eleven beds

but round nearly every tree, and then waited in great agitation for the promised paradise to appear. It did not, and I learned my first lesson.

Luckily I had sown two great patches of sweet-peas which made me very happy all the summer, and then there were some sun-flowers and a few hollyhocks under the south windows, with Madonna lilies in between. But the lilies, after being transplanted, dis-appeared to my great dismay, for how was I to know it was the way of lilies ? And the hollyhocks turned out to be rather ugly colours, so that my first summer was deco-rated and beautified solely by sweet-peas.

At present we are only just beginning to breathe after the bustle of getting new beds and borders and paths made in time for this summer. The eleven beds round the sun-dial are filled with roses, but I see already that I have made mistakes with some. As I have not a living soul with whom to hold communion on this or indeed on any matter, my only way of learning is by making mis-takes. All eleven were to have been car-

peted with purple pansies, but finding that
I had not enough and that nobody had any
to sell me, only six have got their pansies, the
others being sown with dwarf mignonette.
Two of the eleven are filled with Marie vàn
Houtte roses, two with Viscountess Folke-
stone, two with Laurette Messimy, one with
Souvenir de la Malmaison, one with Adam
and Devoniensis, two with Persian Yellow
and Bicolor, and one big bed behind the sun-
dial with three sorts of red roses (seventy-
two in all), Duke of Teck, Cheshunt Scarlet,
and Prefet de Limburg.   This bed is, I am
sure, a mistake, and several of the others
are, I think, but of course I must wait and
see, being such an ignorant person.   Then I
have had two long beds made in the grass on
either side of the semicircle, each sown with
mignonette, and one filled with Marie van
Houtte, and the other with Jules Finger and
the Bride ;   and in a warm corner under the
drawing-room windows is a bed of Madame
Lambard, Madame de Watteville, and Com-
tesse Riza du Parc ;   while farther down the
garden, sheltered on the north and west by a

group of beeches and lilacs, is another large bed, containing Rubens, Madame Joseph Schwartz, and the Hon. Edith Gifford. All these roses are dwarf; I have only two standards in the whole garden, two Madame George Bruants, and they look like broomsticks. How I long for the day when the teas open their buds! Never did I look forward so intensely to anything; and every day I go the rounds, admiring what the dear little things have achieved in the twenty-four hours in the way of new leaf or increase of lovely red shoot.

The hollyhocks and lilies (now flourishing) are still under the south windows in a narrow border on the top of a grass slope, at the foot of which I have sown two long borders of sweet-peas facing the rose beds, so that my roses may have something almost as sweet as themselves to look at until the autumn, when everything is to make place for more tea-roses. The path leading away from this semicircle down the garden is bordered with China roses, white and pink, with here and there a Persian Yellow. I wish now I had put teas there, and I have misgivings as to the effect of the Persian Yellows among the Chinas, for the Chinas are such wee little baby things, and the Persian Yellows look as though they intended to be big bushes.

There is not a creature in all this part of the world who could in the least understand with what heart-beatings I am looking forward to the flowering of these roses, and not a German gardening book that does not relegate all teas to hot-houses, imprisoning them for life, and depriving them for ever of the breath of God. It was no doubt because I was so ignorant that I rushed in where Teutonic angels fear to tread and made my teas face a northern winter; but they did face it under fir branches and leaves, and not one has suffered, and they are looking to-day as happy and as determined to enjoy themselves as any roses, I am sure, in Europe.

May 14*th*.—To-day I am writing on the verandah with the three babies, more persistent than mosquitoes, raging round me, and already several of the thirty fingers

have been in the ink-pot and the owners consoled when duty pointed to rebukes. But
who can rebuke such penitent and drooping
sunbonnets ? I can see nothing but sunbonnets and pinafores and nimble black legs.

These three, their patient nurse, myself,
the gardener, and the gardener's assistant,
are the only people who ever go into my
garden, but then neither are we ever out of
it. The gardener has been here a year and
has given me notice regularly on the first of
every month, but up to now has been induced
to stay on. On the first of this month he
came as usual, and with determination
written on every feature told me he intended
to go in June, and that nothing should alter
his decision. I don't think he knows much
about gardening, but he can at least dig and
water, and some of the things he sows come
up, and some of the plants he plants grow,
besides which he is the most unflaggingly
industrious person I ever saw, and has the
great merit of never appearing to take the
faintest interest in what we do in the garden.
So I have tried to keep him on, not knowing

what the next one may be like, and when I asked him what he had to complain of and he replied " Nothing," I could only conclude that he has a personal objection to me because of my eccentric preference for plants in groups rather than plants in lines. Perhaps, too, he does not like the extracts from gardening books I read to him sometimes when he is planting or sowing something new. Being so helpless myself I thought it simpler, instead of explaining, to take the book itself out to him and let him have wisdom at its very source, administering it in doses while he worked. I quite recognise that this must be annoying, and only my anxiety not to lose a whole year through some stupid mistake has given me the courage to do it. I laugh sometimes behind the book at his disgusted face, and wish we could be photographed, so that I may be reminded in twenty years' time, when the garden is a bower of loveliness and I learned in all its ways, of my first happy struggles and failures.

All through April he was putting the

perennials we had sown in the autumn into
their permanent places, and all through
April he went about with a long piece of
string making parallel lines down the borders
of beautiful exactitude and arranging the
poor plants like soldiers at a review. Two
long borders were done during my absence
one day, and when I explained that I should
like the third to have plants in groups and
not in lines, and that what I wanted was a
natural effect with no bare spaces of earth to
be seen, he looked even more gloomily hope-
less than usual; and on my going out later
on to see the result, I found he had planted
two long borders down the sides of a straight
walk with little lines of five plants in a row—
first five pinks, and next to them five rockets,
and behind the rockets five pinks, and behind the pinks five rockets, and so on with
different plants of every sort and size down
to the end. When I protested, he said he
had only carried out my orders and had
known it would not look well; so I gave in,
and the remaining borders were done after
the pattern of the first two, and I will have

patience and see how they look this summer, before digging them up again; for it becomes beginners to be humble.

If I could only dig and plant myself! How much easier, besides being so fascinating, to make your own holes exactly where you want them and put in your plants exactly as you choose instead of giving orders that can only be half understood from the moment you depart from the lines laid down by that long piece of string! In the first ecstasy of having a garden all my own, and in my burning impatience to make the waste places blossom like a rose, I did one warm Sunday in last year's April during the servants' dinner hour, doubly secure from the gardener by the day and the dinner, slink out with a spade and a rake and feverishly dig a little piece of ground and break it up and sow surreptitious ipomæa and run back very hot and guilty into the house and get into a chair and behind a book and look languid just in time to save my reputation. And why not? It is not graceful, and it makes one hot; but it is a blessed sort of work, and if Eve had had a spade in Paradise and known what to do with it, we should not have had all that sad business of the apple.

What a happy woman I am living in a garden, with books, babies, birds, and flowers, and plenty of leisure to enjoy them! Yet my town acquaintances look upon it as imprisonment, and burying, and I don't know what besides, and would rend the air with their shrieks if condemned to such a life. Sometimes I feel as if I were blest above all my fellows in being able to find my happiness so easily. I believe I should always be good if the sun always shone, and could enjoy myself very well in Siberia on a fine day. And what can life in town offer in the way of pleasure to equal the delight of any one of the calm evenings I have had this month sitting alone at the foot of the verandah steps, with the perfume of young larches all about, and the May moon hanging low over the beeches, and the beautiful silence made only more profound in its peace by the croaking of distant frogs and

the hooting of owls?   A cockchafer darting
by close to my ear with a loud hum sends a
shiver through me, partly of pleasure at the
reminder of past summers, and partly of fear
lest he should get caught in my hair.   The
Man of Wrath says they are pernicious
creatures and should be killed.   I would
rather get the killing done at the end of the
summer and not crush them out of such a
pretty world at the very beginning of all the
fun.

This has been quite an eventful afternoon.
My eldest baby, born in April, is five years
old, and the youngest, born in June, is
three ; so that the discerning will at once be
able to guess the age of the remaining middle
or May baby.   While I was stooping over a
group of hollyhocks planted on the top of
the only thing in the shape of a hill the
garden possesses, the April baby, who had
been sitting pensive on a tree stump close by,
got up suddenly and began to run aimlessly
about, shrieking and wringing her hands
with every symptom of terror.   I stared,
wondering what had come to her ; and then

I saw that a whole army of young cows, pasturing in a field next to the garden, had got through the hedge and were grazing perilously near my tea-roses and most precious belongings. The nurse and I managed to chase them away, but not before they had trampled down a border of pinks and lilies in the cruellest way, and made great holes in a bed of China roses, and even begun to nibble at a Jackmanni clematis that I am trying to persuade to climb up a tree trunk. The gloomy gardener happened to be ill in bed, and the assistant was at vespers—as Lutheran Germany calls afternoon tea or its equivalent—so the nurse filled up the holes as well as she could with mould, burying the crushed and mangled roses, cheated for ever of their hopes of summer glory, and I stood by looking on dejectedly. The June baby, who is two feet square and valiant beyond her size and years, seized a stick much bigger than herself and went after the cows, the cowherd being nowhere to be seen. She planted herself in front of them brandishing her stick, and they stood in a row and stared at her in great astonishment; and she kept them off until one of the men from the farm arrived with a whip, and having found the cowherd sleeping peacefully in the shade, gave him a sound beating. The cowherd is a great hulking young man, much bigger than the man who beat him, but he took his punishment as part of the day's work and made no remark of any sort. It could not have hurt him much through his leather breeches, and I think he deserved it; but it must be demoralising work for a strong young man with no brains looking after cows. Nobody with less imagination than a poet ought to take it up as a profession.

After the June baby and I had been welcomed back by the other two with as many hugs as though we had been restored to them from great perils, and while we were peacefully drinking tea under a beech tree, I happened to look up into its mazy green, and there, on a branch quite close to my head, sat a little baby owl. I got on the seat and caught it easily, for it could not fly, and how it had reached the branch at all is a mystery. It is a little round ball of gray fluff, with the quaintest, wisest, solemn face. Poor thing! I ought to have let it go, but the temptation to keep it until the Man of Wrath, at present on a journey, has seen it was not to be resisted, as he has often said how much he would like to have a young owl and try and tame it. So I put it into a roomy cage and slung it up on a branch near where it had been sitting, and which cannot be far from its nest and its mother. We had hardly subsided again to our tea when I saw two more balls of fluff on the ground in the long grass and scarcely distinguishable at a little distance from small mole-hills. These were promptly united to their relation in the cage, and now when the Man of Wrath comes home, not only shall he be welcomed by a wife wreathed in the orthodox smiles, but by the three little longed-for owls. Only it seems wicked to take them from their mother, and I know that I shall let them go again some day—perhaps the very next time the Man of Wrath goes on a journey.

I put a small pot of water in the cage, though they never could have tasted water yet unless they drink the raindrops off the beech leaves. I suppose they get all the liquid they need from the bodies of the mice and other dainties provided for them by their fond parents. But the raindrop idea is prettier.

May 15*th.*—How cruel it was of me to put those poor little owls into a cage even for one night! I cannot forgive myself, and shall never pander to the Man of Wrath's wishes again. This morning I got up early to see how they were getting on, and I found the door of the cage wide open and no owls to be seen. I thought of course that somebody had stolen them—some boy from the village, or perhaps the chastised cowherd. But looking about I saw one perched high up in the branches of the beech tree, and then to my dismay one lying dead on the ground. The third was nowhere to be seen, and is probably safe in its nest. The parents must have torn at the bars of the cage until by chance they got the door open, and then dragged the little ones out and up into the tree. The one that is dead must have been blown off the branch, as it was a windy night and its neck is broken. There is one happy life less in the garden to-day through my fault, and it is such a lovely, warm day— just the sort of weather for young soft things to enjoy and grow in. The babies are greatly distressed, and are digging a grave, and preparing funeral wreaths of dandelions.

Just as I had written that I heard sounds of arrival, and running out I breathlessly told the Man of Wrath how nearly I had been able to give him the owls he has so often said he would like to have, and how sorry I was they were gone, and how grievous the death of one, and so on after the voluble manner of women.

He listened till I paused to breathe, and then he said, "I am surprised at such cruelty. How could you make the mother owl suffer so? She had never done you any harm."

Which sent me out of the house and into

the garden more convinced than ever that he sang true who sang—

Two paradises 'twere in one to live in Paradise alone.

May 16*th*.—The garden is the place I go to for refuge and shelter, not the house. In the house are duties and annoyances, servants to exhort and admonish, furniture, and meals ; but out there blessings crowd round me at every step—it is there that I am sorry for the unkindness in me, for those selfish thoughts that are so much worse than they feel, it is there that all my sins and silliness are forgiven, there that I feel protected and at home, and every flower and weed is a friend and every tree a lover. When I have been vexed I run out to them for comfort, and when I have been angry without just cause, it is there that I find absolution. Did ever a woman have so many friends ? And always the same, always ready to welcome me and fill me with cheerful thoughts. Happy children of a common Father, why should I, their own sister, be less content and joyous than they ? Even in a thunder-

storm when other people are running into
the house I run out of it. I do not like
thunderstorms—they frighten me for hours
before they come, because I always feel them
on the way; but it is odd that I should go
for shelter to the garden. I feel better there,
more taken care of, more petted. When it
thunders, the April baby says, " There's
lieber Gott scolding those angels again."
And once, when there was a storm in the
night, she complained loudly and wanted to
know why *lieber Gott* didn't do the scolding
in the daytime, as she had been so *tight*
asleep. They all three speak a wonderful
mixture of German and English, adulterating
the purity of their native tongue by putting
in English words in the middle of a German
sentence. It always reminds me of Justice
tempered by Mercy.

We have been cowslipping to-day in a
little wood dignified by the name of the
Hirschwald, because it is the happy hunting-
ground of innumerable deer who fight there
in the autumn evenings, calling each other
out to combat with bayings that ring

through the silence and send agreeable shivers through the lonely listener. I often walk there in September, late in the evening, and sitting on a fallen tree listen fascinated to their angry cries.

We made cowslip balls sitting on the grass. The babies had never seen such things nor had imagined anything half so sweet. The Hirschwald is a little open wood of silver birches and springy turf starred with flowers, and there is a tiny stream meandering amiably about it and decking itself in June with yellow flags. I have dreams of having a little cottage built there, with the daisies up to the door, and no path of any sort—just big enough to hold myself and one baby inside and a purple clematis outside. Two rooms—a bedroom and a kitchen. How scared we would be at night, and how completely happy by day! I know the exact spot where it should stand, facing south-east, so that we should get all the cheerfulness of the morning, and close to the stream, so that we might wash our plates among the flags. Sometimes, when in the mood for society, we would invite the remaining babies to tea and entertain them with wild strawberries on plates of horse-chestnut leaves ; but no one less innocent and easily pleased than a baby would be permitted to darken the effulgence of our sunny cottage—indeed, I don't suppose that anybody wiser would care to come. Wise people want so many things before they can even begin to enjoy themselves, and I feel perpetually apologetic when with them, for only being able to offer them that which I love best myself—apologetic, and ashamed of being so easily contented.

The other day at a dinner party in the nearest town (it took us the whole afternoon to get there) the women after dinner were curious to know how I had endured the winter, cut off from everybody and snowed up sometimes for weeks.

"Ah, these husbands ! " sighed an ample lady, lugubriously shaking her head, " they shut up their wives because it suits them, and don't care what their sufferings are."

Then the others sighed and shook their

heads too, for the ample lady was a great local potentate, and one began to tell how another dreadful husband had brought his young wife into the country and had kept her there, concealing her beauty and accomplishments from the public in a most cruel manner, and how, after spending a certain number of years in alternately weeping and producing progeny, she had quite lately run away with somebody unspeakable —I think it was the footman, or the baker, or some one of that sort.

" But I am quite happy," I began, as soon as I could put in a word.

" Ah, a good little wife, making the best of it," and the female potentate patted my hand, but continued to gloomily shake her head.

" You cannot possibly be happy in the winter entirely alone," asserted another lady, the wife of a high military authority and not accustomed to be contradicted.

" But I am."

" But how can you possibly be at your age? No, it is not possible."

" But I *am*."

" Your husband ought to bring you to town in the winter."

" But I don't want to be brought to town."

" And not let you waste your best years buried."

" But I like being buried."

" Such solitude is not right."

" But I'm not solitary."

" And can come to no good."   She was getting quite angry.

There was a chorus of No Indeeds at her last remark, and renewed shaking of heads.

" I enjoyed the winter immensely," I persisted when they were a little quieter ; " I sleighed and skated, and then there were the children, and shelves and shelves full of —— " I was going to say books, but stopped. Reading is an occupation for men ; for women it is reprehensible waste of time. And how could I talk to them of the happiness I felt when the sun shone on the snow, or of the deep delight of hoar-frost days ?

" It is entirely my doing that we have

come down here," I proceeded, " and my husband only did it to please me."

" Such a good little wife," repeated the patronising potentate, again patting my hand with an air of understanding all about it, " really an excellent little wife. But you must not let your husband have his own way too much, my dear, and take my advice and insist on his bringing you to town next winter."

And then they fell to talking about their cooks, having settled to their entire satisfaction that my fate was probably lying in wait for me too, lurking perhaps at that very moment behind the apparently harmless brass buttons of the man in the hall with my cloak.

I laughed on the way home, and I laughed again for sheer satisfaction when we reached the garden and drove between the quiet trees to the pretty old house ; and when I went into the library, with its four windows open to the moonlight and the scent, and looked round at the familiar bookshelves, and could hear no sounds but sounds of peace, and knew that here I might read or dream or idle exactly as I chose with never a creature to disturb me, how grateful I felt to the kindly Fate that has brought me here and given me a heart to understand my own blessedness, and rescued me from a life like that I had just seen—a life spent with the odours of other people's dinners in one's nostrils, and the noise of their wrangling servants in one's ears, and parties and tattle for all amusement.

But I must confess to having felt some-times quite crushed when some grand person, examining the details of my home through her eyeglass, and coolly dissecting all that I so much prize from the convenient distance of the open window, has finished up by expressing sympathy with my loneliness, and on my protesting that I like it, has murmured, " *sehr anspruchslos*." Then I have felt ashamed of the fewness of my wants ; but only for a moment, and only under the withering influence of the eye-glass ; for, after all, the owner's spirit is the same spirit as that which dwells in my servants—girls whose one idea of happiness is to live in a town where there are others of their sort with whom to drink beer and dance on Sunday afternoons. The passion for being for ever with one's fellows, and the fear of being left for a few hours alone, is to me wholly incomprehensible. I can entertain myself quite well for weeks together, hardly aware, except for the pervading peace, that I have been alone at all. Not but what I like to have people staying with me for a few days, or even for a few weeks, should they be as *anspruchslos* as I am myself, and content with simple joys ; only, any one who comes here and would be happy must have something in him ; if he be a mere blank creature, empty of head and heart, he will very probably find it dull. I should like my house to be often full if I could find people capable of enjoying themselves. They should be welcomed and sped with equal heartiness ; for truth compels me to confess that, though it pleases me to see them come, it pleases me just as much to see them go.

On some very specially divine days, like
to-day, I have actually longed for some one
else to be here to enjoy the beauty with me.
There has been rain in the night, and the
whole garden seems to be singing—not the
untiring birds only, but the vigorous plants,
the happy grass and trees, the lilac bushes
—oh, those lilac bushes ! They are all out
to-day, and the garden is drenched with
the scent. I have brought in armfuls, the
picking is such a delight, and every pot and
bowl and tub in the house is filled with
purple glory, and the servants think there
is going to be a party and are extra nimble,
and I go from room to room gazing at the
sweetness, and the windows are all flung
open so as to join the scent within to the
scent without ; and the servants gradually
discover that there is no party, and wonder
why the house should be filled with flowers
for one woman by herself, and I long more
and more for a kindred spirit—it seems so
greedy to have so much loveliness to oneself
—but kindred spirits are so very, very rare ;
I might almost as well cry for the moon. It

is true that my garden is full of friends, only they are—dumb.

June 3rd.—This is such an out-of-the-way corner of the world that it requires quite unusual energy to get here at all, and I am thus delivered from casual callers ; while, on the other hand, people I love, or people who love me, which is much the same thing, are not likely to be deterred from coming by the roundabout train journey and the long drive at the end. Not the least of my many blessings is that we have only one neighbour. If you have to have neighbours at all, it is at least a mercy that there should be only one ; for with people dropping in at all hours and wanting to talk to you, how are you to get on with your life, I should like to know, and read your books, and dream your dreams to your satisfaction ? Besides, there is always the certainty that either you or the dropper-in will say something that would have been better left unsaid, and I have a holy horror of gossip and mischief-making. A woman's tongue is a deadly weapon and the most difficult thing in the world to keep in order, and things slip off it with a facility nothing short of appalling at the very moment when it ought to be most quiet. In such cases the only safe course is to talk steadily about cooks and children, and to pray that the visit may not be too prolonged, for if it is you are lost. Cooks I have found to be the best of all subjects—the most phlegmatic flush into life at the mere word, and the joys and sufferings connected with them are experiences common to us all.

Luckily, our neighbour and his wife are both busy and charming, with a whole troop of flaxen-haired little children to keep them occupied, besides the business of their large estate. Our intercourse is arranged on lines of the most beautiful simplicity. I call on her once a year, and she returns the call a fortnight later; they ask us to dinner in the summer, and we ask them to dinner in the winter. By strictly keeping to this, we avoid all danger of that closer friendship which is only another name for frequent quarrels. She is a pattern of what a German country lady should be, and is not only a pretty woman but an energetic and practical one, and the combination is, to say the least, effective. She is up at daylight superintending the feeding of the stock, the butter-making, the sending off of the milk for sale ; a thousand things get done while most people are fast asleep, and before lazy folk are well at breakfast she is off in her pony-carriage to the other farms on the place, to rate the " mamsells," as the head women are called, to poke into every corner, lift the lids off the saucepans, count the new-laid eggs, and box, if necessary, any careless dairymaid's ears. We are allowed by law to administer " slight corporal punishment " to our servants, it being left entirely to individual taste to decide what " slight " shall be, and my neighbour really seems to enjoy using this privilege, judging from the way she talks about it. I would give much to be able to peep through a keyhole and see the dauntless little lady, terrible in her wrath and dignity, standing on tiptoe to box the ears of some great strapping girl big enough to eat her.

The making of cheese and butter and sausages *excellently* well is a work which requires brains, and is, to my thinking, a very admirable form of activity, and entirely worthy of the attention of the intelligent. That my neighbour is intelligent is at once made evident by the bright alertness of her eyes—eyes that nothing escapes, and that only gain in prettiness by being used to some good purpose. She is a recognised authority for miles around on the mysteries of sausage-making, the care of calves, and the slaughtering of swine; and with all her manifold duties and daily prolonged absences from home, her children are patterns of health and neatness, and of what dear little German children, with white pigtails and fearless eyes and thick legs, should be. Who shall say that such a life is sordid and dull and unworthy of a high order of intelligence ? I protest that to me it is a beautiful life, full of wholesome outdoor work, and with no room for those listless

moments of depression and boredom, and
of wondering what you will do next, that
leave wrinkles round a pretty woman's eyes,
and are not unknown even to the most
brilliant. But while admiring my neighbour,
I don't think I shall ever try to follow in her
steps, my talents not being of the energetic
and organising variety, but rather of that
order which makes their owner almost
lamentably prone to take up a volume of
poetry and wander out to where the king-
cups grow, and, sitting on a willow trunk
beside a little stream, forget the very existence of everything but green pastures and
still waters, and the glad blowing of the
wind across the joyous fields. And it would
make me perfectly wretched to be confronted by ears so refractory as to require
boxing.

Sometimes callers from a distance invade
my solitude, and it is on these occasions
that I realise how absolutely alone each
individual is, and how far away from his
neighbour, and while they talk (generally
about babies, past, present, and to come),

I fall to wondering at the vast and impass-able distance that separates one's own soul from the soul of the person sitting in the next chair. I am speaking of comparative strangers, people who are forced to stay a certain time by the eccentricities of trains, and in whose presence you grope about after common interests and shrink back into your shell on finding that you have none. Then a frost slowly settles down on me and I grow each minute more benumbed and speechless, and the babies feel the frost in the air and look vacant, and the callers go through the usual form of wondering who they most take after, generally settling the question by saying that the May baby, who is the beauty, is like her father, and that the two more or less plain ones are the image of me, and this decision, though I know it of old and am sure it is coming, never fails to depress me as much as though I heard it for the first time. The babies are very little and inoffensive and good, and it is hard that they should be used as a means of filling up gaps in conversation, and their

features pulled to pieces one by one, and
all their weak points noted and criticised,
while they stand smiling shyly in the
operator's face, their very smile drawing
forth comments on the shape of their
mouths; but, after all, it does not occur
very often, and they are one of those few
interests one has in common with other
people, as everybody seems to have babies.
A garden, I have discovered, is by no means
a fruitful topic, and it is amazing how few
persons really love theirs—they all pretend
they do, but you can hear by the very tone
of their voice what a lukewarm affection it
is. About June their interest is at its
warmest, nourished by agreeable supplies of
strawberries and roses, but on reflection I
don't know a single person within twenty
miles who really cares for his garden, or has
discovered the treasures of happiness that
are buried in it, and are to be found if sought
for diligently, and if needs be with tears.

It is after these rare calls that I experience
the only moments of depression from which
I ever suffer, and then I am angry at myself,

a well-nourished person, for allowing even
a single precious hour of life to be spoilt by
anything so indifferent. That is the worst
of being fed enough and clothed enough
and warmed enough and of having everything you can reasonably desire — on the
least provocation you are made uncomfortable and unhappy by such abstract dis-
comforts as being shut out from a nearer
approach to your neighbour's soul ; which
is on the face of it foolish, the probability
being that he hasn't got one.

The rockets are all out. The gardener
in a fit of inspiration put them right along
the very front of two borders, and I don't
know what his feelings can be now that
they are all flowering and the plants behind
are completely hidden ; but I have learned
another lesson and no future gardener shall
be allowed to run riot among my rockets
in quite so reckless a fashion. They are
charming things, as delicate in colour as in
scent, and a bowl of them on my writing-
table fills the room with fragrance. Single
rows, however, are a mistake ; I had masses

of them planted in the grass, and these show
how lovely they can be. A border full of
rockets, mauve and white, and nothing else,
must be beautiful; but I don't know how
long they last nor what they look like when
they have done flowering. This I shall find
out in a week or two, I suppose. Was ever
a would-be gardener left so entirely to his
own blunderings? No doubt it would be
a gain of years to the garden if I were not
forced to learn solely by my failures, and if
I had some kind creature to tell me when
to do things. At present the only flowers
in the garden are the rockets, the pansies
in the rose beds, and two groups of azaleas—
mollis and pontica. The azaleas have been
and still are gorgeous; I only planted them
this spring and they almost at once began
to flower, and the sheltered corner they
are in looks as though it were filled with
imprisoned and perpetual sunsets. Orange,
lemon, pink in every delicate shade—what
they will be next year and in succeeding
years when the bushes are bigger I can
imagine from the way they have begun life.

On gray, dull days the effect is absolutely startling. Next autumn I shall make a great bank of them in front of a belt of fir trees in rather a gloomy nook. My tea-roses are covered with buds which will not open for at least another week, so I conclude this is not the sort of climate where they will flower from the very beginning of June to November, as they are said to do.

July 11*th*.—There has been no rain since the day before Whitsunday, five weeks ago, which partly, but not entirely, accounts for the disappointment my beds have been. The dejected gardener went mad soon after Whitsuntide and had to be sent to an asylum. He took to going about with a spade in one hand and a revolver in the other, explaining that he felt safer that way, and we bore it quite patiently, as becomes civilised beings who respect each other's prejudices, until one day, when I mildly asked him to tie up a fallen creeper—and after he bought the revolver my tones in addressing him were of the mildest, and I quite left off reading to him aloud—he turned round, looked me straight in the face for the first time since he has been here, and said, "Do I look like Graf X—— (a great local celebrity), or like a monkey?" After which there was nothing for it but to get him into an asylum as expeditiously as possible. There was no gardener to be had in his place, and I have only just succeeded in getting one; so that what with the drought, and the neglect, and the gardener's madness, and my blunders, the garden is in a sad condition; but even in a sad condition it is the dearest place in the world, and all my mistakes only make me more determined to persevere.

The long borders, where the rockets were, are looking dreadful. The rockets have done flowering, and, after the manner of rockets in other walks of life, have degenerated into sticks; and nothing else in those borders intends to bloom this summer. The giant poppies I had planted out in them in April have either died off or remained quite small, and so have the columbines;

here and there a delphinium droops un-
willingly, and that is all. I suppose poppies
cannot stand being moved, or perhaps they
were not watered enough at the time of
transplanting ; anyhow, those borders are
going to be sown to-morrow with more
poppies for next year ; for poppies I will
have, whether they like it or not, and they
shall not be touched, only thinned out.

Well, it is no use being grieved, and after
all, directly I come out and sit under the
trees, and look at the dappled sky, and see
the sunshine on the cornfields away on the
plain, all the disappointment smooths itself
out, and it seems impossible to be sad and
discontented when everything about me is so
radiant and kind.

To-day is Sunday, and the garden is so
quiet, that, sitting here in this shady corner
watching the lazy shadows stretching themselves across the grass, and listening to the
rooks quarrelling in the tree-tops, I almost
expect to hear English church bells ringing
for the afternoon service. But the church
is three miles off, has no bells, and no after-

noon service. Once a fortnight we go to morning prayer at eleven and sit up in a sort of private box with a room behind, whither we can retire unobserved when the sermon is too long or our flesh too weak, and hear ourselves being prayed for by the black-robed parson. In winter the church is bitterly cold; it is not heated, and we sit muffled up in more furs than ever we wear out of doors; but it would of course be very wicked for the parson to wear furs, however cold he may be, so he puts on a great many extra coats under his gown, and, as the winter progresses, swells to a prodigious size. We know when spring is coming by the reduction in his figure. The congregation sit at ease while the parson does the praying for them, and while they are droning the long-drawn-out chorales, he retires into a little wooden box just big enough to hold him. He does not come out until he thinks we have sung enough, nor do we stop until his appearance gives us the signal. I have often thought how dreadful it would be if he fell ill in his box and left us to go on singing. I am sure we should never dare to stop, unauthorised by the Church. I asked him once what he did in there : he looked very shocked at such a profane question, and made an evasive reply.

If it were not for the garden, a German Sunday would be a terrible day ; but in the garden on that day there is a sigh of relief and more profound peace, nobody raking or sweeping or fidgeting ; only the little flowers themselves and the whispering trees.

I have been much afflicted again lately by visitors—not stray callers to be got rid of after a due administration of tea and things you are sorry afterwards that you said, but people staying in the house and not to be got rid of at all. All June was lost to me in this way, and it was from first to last a radiant month of heat and beauty ; but a garden where you meet the people you saw at breakfast, and will see again at lunch and dinner, is not a place to be happy in. Besides, they had a knack of finding out my favourite seats and lounging in them just when I longed to lounge myself ; and they took books out of the library with them, and left them face downwards on the seats all night to get well drenched with dew, though they might have known that what is meat for roses is poison for books ; and they gave me to understand that if they had had the arranging of the garden it would have been finished long ago — whereas I don't believe a garden ever is finished. They have all gone now, thank heaven, except one, so that I have a little breathing space before others begin to arrive. It seems that the place interests people, and that there is a sort of novelty in staying in such a deserted corner of the world, for they were in a perpetual state of mild amusement at being here at all.

Irais is the only one left. She is a young woman with a beautiful, refined face, and her eyes and straight, fine eyebrows are particularly lovable. At meals she dips her bread into the salt-cellar, bites a bit off, and repeats the process, although providence (taking my shape) has caused salt-spoons to be placed at convenient intervals down the table. She lunched to-day on beer, *Schweinekoteletten*, and cabbage-salad with caraway seeds in it, and now I hear her through the open window, extemporising touching melodies in her charming, cooing voice. She is thin, frail, intelligent, and lovable, all on the above diet. What better proof can be needed to establish the superiority of the Teuton than the fact that after such meals he can produce such music? Cabbage-salad is a horrid invention, but I don't doubt its utility as a means of encouraging thoughtfulness; nor will I quarrel with it, since it results so poetically, any more than I quarrel with the manure that results in roses, and I give it to Irais every day to make her sing. She is the sweetest singer I have ever heard, and has a charming trick of making up songs as she goes along. When she begins, I go and lean out of the window and look at my little friends out there in the borders while listening to her music, and feel full of pleasant sadness and regret. It is so sweet to be sad when one has nothing to be sad about.

The April baby came panting up just as I had written that, the others hurrying along behind, and with flaming cheeks displayed for my admiration three brand-new kittens, lean and blind, that she was carrying in her pinafore, and that had just been found motherless in the wood-shed.

" Look," she cried breathlessly, " such a much ! "

I was glad it was only kittens this time, for she had been once before this afternoon on purpose, as she informed me, sitting herself down on the grass at my feet, to ask about the *lieber Gott*, it being Sunday and her pious little nurse's conversation having run, as it seems, on heaven and angels.

Her questions about the *lieber Gott* are better left unrecorded, and I was relieved when she began about the angels.

" What do they wear for clothes ? " she asked in her German-English.

" Why, you've seen them in pictures," I answered, " in beautiful, long dresses, and with big, white wings."

" Feathers ? " she asked.

" I suppose so,—and long dresses, all white and beautiful."

" Are they girlies ? "

" Girls ?   Ye—es."

" Don't boys go into the *Himmel* ? "

" Yes, of course, if they're good."

" And then what do *they* wear ? "

" Why, the same as all the other angels, I suppose."

" *Dwesses ?* "

She began to laugh, looking at me sideways as though she suspected me of making jokes. " What a funny Mummy ! " she said, evidently much amused. She has a fat little laugh that is very infectious.

" I think," said I gravely, "you had better go and play with the other babies."

She did not answer, and sat still a moment watching the clouds.   I began writing again.

" Mummy," she said presently.

" Well ? "

" Where do the angels get their dwesses?"

I hesitated.   " From *lieber Gott*," I said.

" Are there shops in the *Himmel* ? "

" Shops ?   No."

"But, then, where does *lieber Gott* buy their dwesses?"

"Now run away like a good baby; I'm busy."

"But you said yesterday, when I asked about *lieber Gott*, that you would tell about Him on Sunday, and it *is* Sunday. Tell me a story about Him."

There was nothing for it but resignation, so I put down my pencil with a sigh. "Call the others, then."

She ran away, and presently they all three emerged from the bushes one after the other, and tried all together to scramble on to my knee. The April baby got the knee as she always seems to get everything, and the other two had to sit on the grass.

I began about Adam and Eve, with an eye to future parsonic probings. The April baby's eyes opened wider and wider, and her face grew redder and redder. I was surprised at the breathless interest she took in the story—the other two were tearing up tufts of grass and hardly listening. I had scarcely got to the angels with the flaming swords and announced that that was all, when she burst out, "Now *I'll* tell about it. Once upon a time there was Adam and Eva, and they had *plenty* of clothes, and there was *no* snake, and *lieber Gott wasn't* angry with them, and they could eat as *many* apples as they liked, and was happy for ever and ever —*there* now ! "

She began to jump up and down defiantly on my knee.

" But that's not the story," I said rather helplessly.

" Yes, yes ! It's a much nicelier one ! Now another."

"But these stories are *true*," I said severely; " and it's no use my telling them if you make them up your own way afterwards."

" Another ! another ! " she shrieked, jumping up and down with redoubled energy, all her silvery curls flying.

I began about Noah and the flood.

" Did it rain *so* badly ? " she asked with a face of the deepest concern and interest.

" Yes, all day long and all night long for weeks and weeks——"

" And was everybody so wet ? "

" Yes——"

" But why didn't they open their um-bwellas ? "

Just then I saw the nurse coming out with the tea-tray.

" I'll tell you the rest another time," I said, putting her off my knee, greatly re-lieved ; " you must all go to Anna now and have tea."

" I don't like Anna," remarked the June baby, not having hitherto opened her lips ; " she is a stupid girl."

The other two stood transfixed with horror at this statement, for, besides being naturally extremely polite, and at all times anxious not to hurt any one's feelings, they have been brought up to love and respect their kind little nurse.

The April baby recovered her speech first, and lifting her finger, pointed it at the criminal in just indignation. " Such a child will *never* go into the *Himmel*," she said with great emphasis, and the air of one who delivers judgment.

September 15*th*.—This is the month of quiet days, crimson creepers, and blackberries ; of mellow afternoons in the ripening garden ; of tea under the acacias instead of the too shady beeches ; of wood-fires in the library in the chilly evenings. The babies go out in the afternoon and blackberry in the hedges ; the three kittens, grown big and fat, sit cleaning themselves on the sunny verandah steps ; the Man of Wrath shoots partridges across the distant stubble ; and the summer seems as though it would dream on for ever. It is hard to believe that in three months we shall probably be snowed up and certainly be cold. There is a feeling about this month that reminds me of March and the early days of April, when spring is still hesitating on the threshold and the garden holds its breath in expectation. There is the same mildness in the air, and the sky and grass have the same look as then ; but the leaves tell a different tale, and the reddening creeper on the house is rapidly approaching its last and loveliest glory.

My roses have behaved as well on the whole as was to be expected, and the Viscountess Folkestones and Laurette Messimys have been most beautiful, the latter being quite the loveliest things in the garden, each flower an exquisite loose cluster of coral-pink petals, paling at the base to a yellow-white. I have ordered a hundred standard teas for planting next month, half of which are Viscountess Folkestones, because the teas have such a way of hanging their little heads that one has to kneel down to be able to see them well in the dwarf forms—not but what I entirely approve of kneeling before such perfect beauty, only it dirties one's clothes. So I am going to put standards down each side of the walk under the south windows, and shall have the flowers on a convenient level for worship. My only fear is, that they will stand the winter less well than the dwarf sorts, being so difficult to pack up snugly. The Persian Yellows and Bicolors have been, as I predicted, a mistake among the teas; they only flower twice in the season, and all the rest of the time look dull and moping; and then the Persian Yellows have such an odd smell and so many insects inside them eating them up. I have ordered Safrano tea-roses to put in their place, as they all come out next month and are to be grouped in the grass; and the semicircle being immediately under the windows, besides having the best position in the place, must be reserved solely for my choicest treasures. I have had a great many disappointments, but feel as though I were really beginning to learn. Humility, and the most patient perseverance, seem almost as necessary in gardening as rain and sunshine, and every failure must be used as a stepping-stone to something better.

I had a visitor last week who knows a great deal about gardening and has had much practical experience. When I heard he was coming, I felt I wanted to put my arms right round my garden and hide it from him; but what was my surprise and delight when he said, after having gone all over it, " Well, I think you have done wonders." Dear me, how pleased I was! It was so entirely unexpected, and such a complete novelty after the remarks I have been listening to all the summer. I could have hugged that discerning and indulgent critic, able to look beyond the result to the intention, and appreciating the difficulties of every kind that had been in the way. After that I opened my heart to him, and listened reverently to all he had to say, and treasured up his kind and encouraging advice, and wished he could stay here a whole year and help me through the seasons. But he went, as people one likes always do go, and he was the only guest I have had whose departure made me sorry.

The people I love are always somewhere else and not able to come to me, while I can at any time fill the house with visitors about whom I know little and care less. Perhaps, if I saw more of those absent ones, I would not love them so well—at least, that is what I think on wet days when the wind is howling round the house and all nature is overcome with grief ; and it has actually happened once or twice when great friends have been staying with me that I have wished, when they left, I might not see them again for at least ten years. I suppose the fact is, that no friendship can stand the breakfast test, and here, in the country, we invariably think it our duty to appear at breakfast. Civilisation has done away with curl-papers, yet at that hour the soul of the *Hausfrau* is as tightly screwed up in them as was ever her grandmother's hair ; and though my body comes down mechanically, having been trained that way by punctual parents, my soul never thinks of beginning to wake up for other people till lunch-time, and never does so completely till it has been taken out of doors and aired in the sunshine. Who can begin conventional amiability the first thing in the morning ? It is the hour of savage instincts and natural tendencies ; it is the triumph of the Disagreeable and the Cross. I am convinced that the Muses and the Graces never thought of having breakfast anywhere but in bed.

November 10*th*.—Last night we had ten

degrees of frost (Fahrenheit), and I went out the first thing this morning to see what had become of the tea-roses, and behold, they were wide awake and quite cheerful— covered with rime it is true, but anything but black and shrivelled. Even those in boxes on each side of the verandah steps were perfectly alive and full of buds, and one in particular, a Bouquet d'Or, is a mass of buds and would flower if it could get the least encouragement. I am beginning to think that the tenderness of teas is much exaggerated, and am certainly very glad I had the courage to try them in this northern garden. But I must not fly too boldly in the face of Providence, and have ordered those in the boxes to be taken into the green-house for the winter, and hope the Bouquet d'Or, in a sunny place near the glass, may be induced to open some of those buds. The greenhouse is only used as a refuge, and kept at a temperature just above freezing, and is reserved entirely for such plants as cannot stand the very coldest part of the winter out of doors. I don't use it for growing anything, because I don't love things that will only bear the garden for three or four months in the year and require coaxing and petting for the rest of it. Give me a garden full of strong, healthy creatures, able to stand roughness and cold without dismally giving in and dying. I never could see that delicacy of constitution is pretty, either in plants or women. No doubt there are many lovely flowers to be had by heat and constant coaxing, but then for each of these there are fifty others still lovelier that will gratefully grow in God's wholesome air and are blessed in return with a far greater intensity of scent and colour.

We have been very busy till now getting the permanent beds into order and planting the new tea-roses, and I am looking forward to next summer with more hope than ever in spite of my many failures. I wish the years would pass quickly that will bring my garden to perfection ! The Persian Yellows have gone into their new quarters, and their place is occupied by the tea-rose Safrano ; all the rose beds are carpeted with pansies sown in July and transplanted in October, each bed having a separate colour. The purple ones are the most charming and go well with every rose, but I have white ones with Laurette Messimy, and yellow ones with Safrano, and a new red sort in the big centre bed of red roses. Round the semicircle on the south side of the little privet hedge two rows of annual larkspurs in all their delicate shades have been sown, and just beyond the larkspurs, on the grass, is a semicircle of standard tea and pillar roses. In front of the house the long borders have been stocked with larkspurs, annual and perennial, columbines, giant poppies, pinks, Madonna lilies, wallflowers, hollyhocks, perennial phloxes, peonies, lavender, starworts, cornflowers, Lychnis chalcedonica, and bulbs packed in wherever bulbs could go. These are the borders that were so hardly used by the other gardener. The spring boxes for the verandah steps have been filled with pink and white and yellow tulips. I love tulips better than any other spring flower; they are the embodiment of alert cheerfulness and tidy grace, and next to a hyacinth look

like a wholesome, freshly tubbed young girl
beside a stout lady whose every movement
weighs down the air with patchouli. Their
faint, delicate scent is refinement itself; and
is there anything in the world more charming
than the sprightly way they hold up their
little faces to the sun? I have heard them
called bold and flaunting, but to me they
seem modest grace itself, only always on the
alert to enjoy life as much as they can and
not afraid of looking the sun or anything else
above them in the face. On the grass there
are two beds of them carpeted with forget-
me-nots; and in the grass, in scattered
groups, are daffodils and narcissus. Down
the wilder shrubbery walks foxgloves and
mulleins will (I hope) shine majestic; and
one cool corner, backed by a group of firs, is
graced by Madonna lilies, white foxgloves,
and columbines. In a distant glade I have
made a spring garden round an oak tree that
stands alone in the sun—groups of crocuses,
daffodils, narcissus, hyacinths, and tulips,
among such flowering shrubs and trees
as Pirus Malus spectabilis, floribunda, and

coronaria; Prunus Juliana, Mahaleb, sero-
tina, triloba, and Pissardi; Cydonias and
Weigelias in every colour, and several kinds
of Cratægus and other May lovelinesses. If
the weather behaves itself nicely, and we
get gentle rains in due season, I think this
little corner will be beautiful—but what a
big " if " it is! Drought is our great enemy,
and the two last summers each contained
five weeks of blazing, cloudless heat when
all the ditches dried up and the soil was like
hot pastry. At such times the watering is
naturally quite beyond the strength of two
men; but as a garden is a place to be happy
in, and not one where you want to meet a
dozen curious eyes at every turn, I should
not like to have more than these two, or
rather one and a half—the assistant having
stork-like proclivities and going home in the
autumn to his native Russia, returning in
the spring with the first warm winds. I
want to keep him over the winter, as there
is much to be done even then, and I sounded
him on the point the other day. He is the
most abject-looking of human beings—lame,

and afflicted with a hideous eye-disease; but he is a good worker and plods along unwearyingly from sunrise to dusk.

" Pray, my good stork," said I, or German words to that effect, " why don't you stay here altogether, instead of going home and rioting away all you have earned ? "

" I would stay," he answered, " but I have my wife there in Russia."

" Your wife ! " I exclaimed, stupidly surprised that the poor deformed creature should have found a mate—as though there were not a superfluity of mates in the world —" I didn't know you were married ? "

" Yes, and I have two little children, and I don't know what they would do if I were not to come home. But it is a very expensive journey to Russia, and costs me every time seven marks."

" Seven marks ! "

" Yes, it is a great sum."

I wondered whether I should be able to get to Russia for seven marks, supposing I were to be seized with an unnatural craving to go there.

All the labourers who work here from
March to December are Russians and Poles,
or a mixture of both. We send a man over
who can speak their language to fetch as
many as he can early in the year, and they
arrive with their bundles, men and women
and babies, and as soon as they have got
here and had their fares paid, they disappear
in the night if they get the chance, sometimes
fifty of them at a time, to go and work singly
or in couples for the peasants, who pay them
a pfenning or two more a day than we do,
and let them eat with the family. From
us they get a mark and a half to two marks
a day and as many potatoes as they can eat.
The women get less, not because they work
less, but because they are women and must
not be encouraged. The overseer lives with
them, and has a loaded revolver in his pocket
and a savage dog at his heels. For the first
week or two after their arrival the foresters
and other permanent officials keep guard
at night over the houses they are put into.
I suppose they find it sleepy work; for
certain it is that spring after spring the same

thing happens, fifty of them getting away in
spite of all our precautions, and we are left
with our mouths open and much out of
pocket.   This spring, by some mistake, they
arrived without their bundles, which had
gone astray on the road, and, as they travel
in their best clothes, they refused utterly
to work until their luggage came.   Nearly
a week was lost waiting, to the despair of
all in authority.

Nor will any persuasions induce them to do
anything on Saints' days, and there surely
never was a church so full of them as the
Russian Church.   In the spring, when every
hour is of vital importance, the work is
constantly being interrupted by them, and
the workers lie sleeping in the sun the whole
day, agreeably conscious that they are
pleasing themselves and the Church at one
and the same time—a state of perfection as
rare as it is desirable.   Reason unaided by
Faith is of course exasperated at this waste
of precious time, and I confess that during
the first mild days after the long winter frost
when it is possible to begin to work the

ground, I have sympathised with the gloom
of the Man of Wrath, confronted in one week
by two or three empty days on which no
man will labour, and have listened in silence
to his remarks about distant Russian saints.

I suppose it was my own superfluous
amount of civilisation that made me pity
these people when first I came to live among
them. They herd together like animals and
do the work of animals ; but in spite of the
armed overseer, the dirt and the rags, the
meals of potatoes washed down by weak
vinegar and water, I am beginning to believe
that they would strongly object to soap, I
am sure they would not wear new clothes,
and I hear them coming home from their
work at dusk singing. They are like little
children or animals in their utter inability
to grasp the idea of a future ; and after all,
if you work all day in God's sunshine, when
evening comes you are pleasantly tired and
ready for rest and not much inclined to find
fault with your lot. I have not yet persuaded myself, however, that the women
are happy. They have to work as hard as

the men and get less for it ; they have to
produce offspring, quite regardless of times
and seasons and the general fitness of things;
they have to do this as expeditiously as
possible, so that they may not unduly
interrupt the work in hand ; nobody helps
them, notices them, or cares about them,
least of all the husband.   It is quite a usual
thing to see them working in the fields in
the morning, and working again in the
afternoon, having in the interval produced
a baby.   The baby is left to an old woman
whose duty it is to look after babies col-
lectively.   When I expressed my horror at
the poor creatures working immediately
afterwards as though nothing had happened,
the Man of Wrath informed me that they
did not suffer because they had never worn
corsets, nor had their mothers and grand-
mothers.   We were riding together at the
time, and had just passed a batch of workers,
and my husband was speaking to the overseer when a woman arrived alone, and taking
up a spade began to dig.   She grinned cheerfully at us as she made a curtsey, and the

overseer remarked that she had just been back to the house and had a baby.

" Poor, *poor* woman ! " I cried, as we rode on, feeling for some occult reason very angry with the Man of Wrath. "And her wretched husband doesn't care a rap, and will probably beat her to-night if his supper isn't right. What nonsense it is to talk about the equality of the sexes when the women have the babies ! "

" Quite so, my dear," replied the Man of Wrath, smiling condescendingly. "You have got to the very root of the matter. Nature, while imposing this agreeable duty on the woman, weakens her and disables her for any serious competition with man. How can a person who is constantly losing a year of the best part of her life compete with a young man who never loses any time at all ? He has the brute force, and his last word on any subject could always be his fist."

I said nothing. It was a dull, gray afternoon in the beginning of November, and the leaves dropped slowly and silently at

our horses' feet as we rode towards the
Hirschwald.

" It is a universal custom," proceeded the
Man of Wrath, " amongst these Russians,
and I believe amongst the lower classes
everywhere, and certainly commendable on
the score of simplicity, to silence a woman's
objections and aspirations by knocking her
down.   I have heard it said that this
apparently brutal action has anything but
the maddening effect tenderly nurtured
persons might suppose, and that the patient
is soothed and satisfied with a rapidity and
completeness unattainable by other and more
polite methods.   Do you suppose," he went
on, flicking a twig off a tree with his whip
as we passed, "that the intellectual husband,
wrestling intellectually with the chaotic
yearnings of his intellectual wife, ever
achieves the result aimed at?   He may and
does go on wrestling till he is tired, but
never does he in the very least convince her
of her folly ; while his brother in the ragged
coat has got through the whole business in
less time than it takes me to speak about it.

There is no doubt that these poor women fulfil their vocation far more thoroughly than the women in our class, and, as the truest happiness consists in finding one's vocation quickly and continuing in it all one's days, I consider they are to be envied rather than not, since they are early taught, by the impossibility of argument with marital muscle, the impotence of female endeavour and the blessings of content."

" Pray go on," I said politely.

" These women accept their beatings with a simplicity worthy of all praise, and far from considering themselves insulted, admire the strength and energy of the man who can administer such eloquent rebukes. In Russia, not only *may* a man beat his wife, but it is laid down in the catechism and taught all boys at the time of confirmation as necessary at least once a week, whether she has done anything or not, for the sake of her general health and happiness."

I thought I observed a tendency in the Man of Wrath to rather gloat over these castigations.

" Pray, my dear man," I said, pointing with my whip, " look at that baby moon so innocently peeping at us over the edge of the mist just behind that silver birch, and don't talk so much about women and things you don't understand. What is the use of your bothering about fists and whips and muscles and all the dreadful things invented for the confusion of obstreperous wives ? You know you are a civilised husband, and a civilised husband is a creature who has ceased to be a man."

" And a civilised wife ? " he asked, bringing his horse close up beside me and putting his arm round my waist, " has she ceased to be a woman ? "

" I should think so indeed, — she is a goddess, and can never be worshipped and adored enough."

" It seems to me," he said, " that the conversation is growing personal."

I started off at a canter. across the short, springy turf. The Hirschwald is an enchanted place on such an evening, when the mists lie low on the turf, and overhead the delicate, bare branches of the silver birches stand out clear against the soft sky, while the little moon looks down kindly on the damp November world. Where the trees thicken into a wood, the fragrance of the wet earth and rotting leaves kicked up by the horses' hoofs fills my soul with delight. I particularly love that smell, — it brings before me the entire benevolence of Nature, for ever working death and decay, so piteous in themselves, into the means of fresh life and glory, and sending up sweet odours as she works.

December 7th.—I have been to England. I went for at least a month and stayed a week in a fog and was blown home again in a gale. Twice I fled before the fogs into the country to see friends with gardens, but it was raining, and except the beautiful lawns (not to be had in the Fatherland) and the infinite possibilities, there was nothing to interest the intelligent and garden-loving foreigner, for the good reason that you cannot be interested in gardens under an umbrella.

So I went back to the fogs, and after groping about for a few days more began to long inordinately for Germany. A terrific gale sprang up after I had started, and the journey both by sea and land was full of horrors, the trains in Germany being heated to such an extent that it is next to impossible to sit still, great gusts of hot air coming up under the cushions, the cushions themselves being very hot and the wretched traveller still hotter.

But when I reached my home and got out of the train into the purest, brightest snow-atmosphere, the air so still that the whole world seemed to be listening, the sky cloudless, the crisp snow sparkling underfoot and on the trees, and a happy row of three beaming babies awaiting me, I was consoled for all my torments, only remembering them enough to wonder why I had gone away at all.

The babies each had a kitten in one hand and an elegant bouquet of pine needles and grass in the other, and what with the due presentation of the bouquets and the struggles of the kittens, the hugging and kissing was

much interfered with. Kittens, bouquets,
and babies were all somehow squeezed into
the sleigh, and off we went with jingling
bells and shrieks of delight.

" Directly you comes home the fun
begins," said the May baby, sitting very
close to me. " How the snow purrs ! "
cried the April baby, as the horses scrunched
it up with their feet. The June baby sat
loudly singing " The King of Love my
Shepherd is," and swinging her kitten round
by its tail to emphasise the rhythm.

The house, half-buried in the snow, looked
the very abode of peace ; and I ran through
all the rooms, eager to take possession of
them again, and feeling as though I had been
away for ever. When I got to the library
I came to a standstill,—ah, the dear room,
what happy times I have spent in it rummag-
ing amongst the books, making plans for
my garden, building castles in the air,
writing, dreaming, doing nothing ! There
was a big peat fire blazing half up the
chimney, and the old housekeeper had put
pots of flowers about, and on the writing-

table was a great bunch of violets scenting the room. " Oh, how *good* it is to be home again ! " I sighed in my satisfaction. The babies clung about my knees, looking up at me with eyes full of love. Outside the dazzling snow and sunshine, inside the bright room and happy faces—I thought of those yellow fogs and shivered.

The library is not used by the Man of Wrath; it is neutral ground where we meet in the evenings for an hour before he disappears into his own rooms — a series of very smoky dens in the south-east corner of the house. It looks, I am afraid, rather too gay for an ideal library; and its colouring, white and yellow, is so cheerful as to be almost frivolous. There are white bookcases all round the walls, and there is a great fireplace, and four windows, facing full south, opening on to my most cherished bit of garden, the bit round the sun-dial; so that with so much colour and such a big fire and such floods of sunshine it has anything but a sober air, in spite of the venerable volumes filling the shelves. Indeed, I

should never be surprised if they skipped
down from their places, and, picking up
their leaves, began to dance.

With this room to live in, I can look
forward with perfect equanimity to being
snowed up for any time Providence thinks
proper ; and to go into the garden in its
snowed-up state is like going into a bath
of purity. The first breath on opening the
door is so ineffably pure that it makes me
gasp, and I feel a black and sinful object
in the midst of all the spotlessness. Yesterday I sat out of doors near the sun-dial the
whole afternoon, with the thermometer so
many degrees below freezing, that it will be
weeks finding its way up again ; but there
was no wind, and beautiful sunshine, and I
was well wrapped up in furs. I even had
tea brought out there, to the astonishment
of the menials, and sat till long after the sun
had set, enjoying the frosty air. I had to
drink the tea very quickly, for it showed a
strong inclination to begin to freeze. After
the sun had gone down the rooks came home
to their nests in the garden with a great

fuss and fluttering, and many hesitations
and squabbles before they settled on their
respective trees. They flew over my head
in hundreds with a mighty swish of wings,
and when they had arranged themselves
comfortably, an intense hush fell upon the
garden, and the house began to look like a
Christmas card, with its white roof against
the clear, pale green of the western sky, and
lamplight shining in the windows.

I had been reading a Life of Luther lent
me by our parson in the intervals between
looking round me and being happy. He
came one day with the book and begged
me to read it, having discovered that my
interest in Luther was not as living as it
ought to be ; so I took it out with me into
the garden, because the dullest book takes
on a certain saving grace if read out of doors,
just as bread and butter, devoid of charm in
the drawing-room, is ambrosia eaten under
a tree. I read Luther all the afternoon with
pauses for refreshing glances at the garden
and the sky, and much thankfulness in my
heart. His struggles with devils amazed

me ; and I wondered whether such a day as that, full of grace and the forgiveness of sins, never struck him as something to make him relent even towards devils. He apparently never allowed himself to just be happy. He was a wonderful man, but I am glad I was not his wife.

Our parson is an interesting person, and untiring in his efforts to improve himself. Both he and his wife study whenever they have a spare moment, and there is a tradition that she stirs her puddings with one hand and holds a Latin grammar in the other, the grammar, of course, getting the greater share of her attention. To most German *Hausfraus* the dinners and the puddings are of paramount importance, and they pride themselves on keeping those parts of their houses that are seen in a state of perpetual and spotless perfection, and this is exceedingly praiseworthy ; but, I would humbly inquire, are there not other things even more important ? And is not plain living and high thinking better than the other way about ? And all too careful making of dinners and dusting of furniture takes a terrible amount of precious time, and — and with shame I confess that my sympathies are all with the pudding and the grammar. It cannot be right to be the slave of one's household gods, and I protest that if my furniture ever annoyed me by wanting to be dusted when I wanted to be doing something else, and there was no one to do the dusting for me, I should cast it all into the nearest bonfire and sit and warm my toes at the flames with great contentment, triumphantly selling my dusters to the very next pedlar who was weak enough to buy them. Parsons' wives have to do the housework and cooking themselves, and are thus not only cooks and housemaids, but if they have children — and they always do have children — they are head and under nurse as well; and besides these trifling duties have a good deal to do with their fruit and vegetable garden, and everything to do with their poultry. This being so, is it not pathetic to find a young woman bravely struggling to learn languages and keep up with her husband? If I were that husband, those puddings would taste sweetest to me that were served with Latin sauce. They are both severely pious, and are for ever engaged in desperate efforts to practise what they preach; than which, as we all know, nothing is more difficult. He works in his parish with the most noble self-devotion, and never loses courage, although his efforts have been several times rewarded by disgusting libels pasted up on the street-corners, thrown under doors, and even fastened to his own garden wall. The peasant hereabouts is past belief low and animal, and a sensitive, intellectual parson among them is really a pearl before swine. For years he has gone on unflinchingly, filled with the most living faith and hope and charity, and I sometimes wonder whether they are any better now in his parish than they were under his predecessor, a man who smoked and drank beer from Monday morning to Saturday night, never did a stroke of work, and often kept the scanty congregation waiting on Sunday afternoons while he finished his post-prandial nap. It is discouraging enough to make most men give in, and leave the parish to get to heaven or not as it pleases; but he never seems discouraged, and goes on sacrificing the best part of his life to these people when all his tastes are literary, and all his inclinations towards the life of the student. His convictions drag him out of his little home at all hours to minister to the sick and exhort the wicked; they give him no rest, and never let him feel he has done enough; and when he comes home weary, after a day's wrestling with his parishioners' souls, he is confronted on his doorstep by filthy abuse pasted up on his own front door. He never speaks of these things, but how shall they be hid ? Everybody here knows everything that happens before the day is over, and what we have for dinner is of far greater general interest than the most astounding political earthquake. They have a pretty, roomy cottage, and a good bit of ground adjoining the churchyard. His predecessor used to hang out his washing on the tombstones to dry, but then he was a person entirely lost to all sense of decency, and had finally to be removed, preaching a farewell sermon of a most vituperative description, and hurling invective at the Man of Wrath, who sat up in his box drinking in every word and enjoying himself thoroughly. The Man of Wrath likes novelty, and such a sermon had never been heard before. It is spoken of in the village to this day with bated breath and awful joy.

December 22nd.—Up to now we have had a beautiful winter. Clear skies, frost, little wind, and, except for a sharp touch now and then, very few really cold days. My windows are gay with hyacinths and lilies of the valley; and though, as I have said, I don't admire the smell of hyacinths in the spring when it seems wanting in youth and chastity next to that of other flowers, I am glad enough now to bury my nose in their heavy sweetness. In December one cannot afford to be fastidious; besides, one is actually less fastidious about everything in the winter.

The keen air braces soul as well as body into robustness, and the food and the perfume disliked in the summer are perfectly welcome then.

I am very busy preparing for Christmas, but have often locked myself up in a room alone, shutting out my unfinished duties, to study the flower catalogues and make my lists of seeds and shrubs and trees for the spring. It is a fascinating occupation, and acquires an additional charm when you know you ought to be doing something else, that Christmas is at the door, that children and servants and farm hands depend on you for their pleasure, and that, if you don't see to the decoration of the trees and house and the buying of the presents, nobody else will. The hours fly by shut up with those catalogues and with Duty snarling on the other side of the door. I don't like Duty—everything in the least disagreeable is always sure to be one's duty. Why cannot it be my duty to make lists and plans for the dear garden ? "And so it *is*," I insisted to the Man of Wrath, when he protested against

what he called wasting my time upstairs.
" No," he replied sagely ; " your garden is
not your Duty, because it is your Pleasure."

What a comfort it is to have such wells of
wisdom constantly at my disposal ! Anybody can have a husband, but to few is it
given to have a sage, and the combination
of both is as rare as it is useful. Indeed, in
its practical utility the only thing I ever saw
to equal it is a sofa my neighbour has bought
as a Christmas surprise for her husband, and
which she showed me the last time I called
there—a beautiful invention, as she explained,
combining a bedstead, a sofa, and a chest of
drawers, and into which you put your clothes,
and on top of which you put yourself, and
if anybody calls in the middle of the night
and you happen to be using the drawing-
room as a bedroom, you just pop the bed-
clothes inside, and there you are discovered
sitting on your sofa and looking for all the
world as though you had been expecting
visitors for hours.

" Pray, does he wear pyjamas ? " I
inquired.

But she had never heard of pyjamas.

It takes a long time to make my spring lists. I want to have a border all yellow, every shade of yellow from fieriest orange to nearly white, and the amount of work and studying of gardening books it costs me will only be appreciated by beginners like myself. I have been weeks planning it, and it is not nearly finished. I want it to be a succession of glories from May till the frosts, and the chief feature is to be the number of " ardent marigolds "—flowers that I very tenderly love—and nasturtiums. The nasturtiums are to be of every sort and shade, and are to climb and creep and grow in bushes, and show their lovely flowers and leaves to the best advantage. Then there are to be eschscholtzias, dahlias, sunflowers, zinnias, scabiosa, portulaca, yellow violas, yellow stocks, yellow sweet - peas, yellow lupins — everything that is yellow or that has a yellow variety. The place I have chosen for it is a long, wide border in the sun, at the foot of a grassy slope crowned with lilacs and pines, and facing south-east.

You go through a little pine wood, and, turning a corner, are to come suddenly upon this bit of captured morning glory. I want it to be blinding in its brightness after the dark, cool path through the wood.

That is the idea. Depression seizes me when I reflect upon the probable difference between the idea and its realisation. I am ignorant, and the gardener is, I do believe, still more so; for he was forcing some tulips, and they have all shrivelled up and died, and he says he cannot imagine why. Besides, he is in love with the cook, and is going to marry her after Christmas, and refuses to enter into any of my plans with the enthusiasm they deserve, but sits with vacant eye dreamily chopping wood from morning till night to keep the beloved one's kitchen fire well supplied. I cannot understand any one preferring cooks to marigolds; those future marigolds, shadowy as they are, and whose seeds are still sleeping at the seedsman's, have shone through my winter days like golden lamps.

I wish with all my heart I were a man, for

of course the first thing I should do would
be to buy a spade and go and garden, and
then I should have the delight of doing
everything for my flowers with my own
hands and need not waste time explaining
what I want done to somebody else. It
is dull work giving orders and trying to
describe the bright visions of one's brain
to a person who has no visions and no
brain, and who thinks a yellow bed should
be calceolarias edged with blue.

I have taken care in choosing my yellow
plants to put down only those humble ones
that are easily pleased and grateful for little,
for my soil is by no means all that it might
be, and to most plants the climate is rather
trying. I feel really grateful to any flower
that is sturdy and willing enough to flourish
here. Pansies seem to like the place and
so do sweet-peas; pinks don't, and after
much coaxing gave hardly any flowers last
summer. Nearly all the roses were a success,
in spite of the sandy soil, except the tea-
rose Adam, which was covered with buds
ready to open, when they suddenly turned

brown and died, and three standard Dr. Grills which stood in a row and simply sulked. I had been very excited about Dr. Grill, his description in the catalogues being specially fascinating, and no doubt I deserved the snubbing I got. " Never be excited, my dears, about *anything*," shall be the advice I will give the three babies when the time comes to take them out to parties, " or, if you are, don't show it. If by nature you are volcanoes, at least be only smouldering ones. Don't look pleased, don't look interested, don't, above all things, look eager. Calm indifference should be written on every feature of your faces. Never show that you like any one person, or any one thing. Be cool, languid, and reserved. If you don't do as your mother tells you and are just gushing, frisky, young idiots, snubs will be your portion. If you do do as she tells you, you'll marry princes and live happily ever after."

Dr. Grill must be a German rose. In this part of the world the more you are pleased to see a person the less is he pleased to see

you ; whereas, if you are disagreeable, he
will grow pleasant visibly, his countenance
expanding into wider amiability the more
your own is stiff and sour. But I was not
prepared for that sort of thing in a rose, and
was disgusted with Dr. Grill. He had the
best place in the garden—warm, sunny, and
sheltered ; his holes were prepared with
the tenderest care ; he was given the most
dainty mixture of compost, clay, and
manure ; he was watered assiduously all
through the drought when more willing
flowers got nothing ; and he refused to do
anything but look black and shrivel. He
did not die, but neither did he live—he just
existed; and at the end of the summer not
one of him had a scrap more shoot or leaf
than when he was first put in in April. It
would have been better if he had died
straight away, for then I should have known
what to do; as it is, there he is still occupying the best place, wrapped up carefully
for the winter, excluding kinder roses, and
probably intending to repeat the same
conduct next year. Well, trials are the

portion of mankind, and gardeners have their share, and in any case it is better to be tried by plants than persons, seeing that with plants you know that it is you who are in the wrong, and with persons it is always the other way about—and who is there among us who has not felt the pangs of injured innocence, and known them to be grievous ?

I have two visitors staying with me, though I have done nothing to provoke such an infliction, and had been looking forward to a happy little Christmas alone with the Man of Wrath and the babies. Fate decreed otherwise. Quite regularly, if I look forward to anything, Fate steps in and decrees otherwise ; I don't know why it should, but it does. I had not even invited these good ladies — like greatness on the modest, they were thrust upon me. One is Irais, the sweet singer of the summer, whom I love as she deserves, but of whom I certainly thought I had seen the last for at least a year, when she wrote and asked if I would have her over Christmas, as her husband was out of sorts, and she didn't like him in that state. Neither do I like sick husbands, so, full of sympathy, I begged her to come, and here she is. And the other is Minora.

Why I have to have Minora I don't know, for I was not even aware of her existence a fortnight ago. Then coming down cheerfully one morning to breakfast—it was the very day after my return from England—I found a letter from an English friend, who up till then had been perfectly innocuous, asking me to befriend Minora. I read the letter aloud for the benefit of the Man of Wrath, who was eating spickgans, a delicacy much sought after in these parts.

"Do, my dear Elizabeth," wrote my friend, "take some notice of the poor thing. She is studying art in Dresden, and has nowhere literally to go for Christmas. She is very ambitious and hardworking——"

"Then," interrupted the Man of Wrath, "she is not pretty. Only ugly girls work hard."

" —and she is really very clever——"

" I do not like clever girls, they are so stupid," again interrupted the Man of Wrath.

" —and unless some kind creature like yourself takes pity on her she will be very lonely."

" Then let her be lonely."

" Her mother is my oldest friend, and would be greatly distressed to think that her daughter should be alone in a foreign town at such a season."

" I do not mind the distress of the mother."

" Oh, dear me," I exclaimed impatiently, " I shall have to ask her to come ! "

" If you *should* be inclined," the letter went on, " to play the good Samaritan, dear Elizabeth, I am positive you would find Minora a bright, intelligent companion——"

" Minora ? " questioned the Man of Wrath.

The April baby, who has had a nursery governess of an altogether alarmingly zealous type attached to her person for the last six weeks, looked up from her bread and milk.

" It sounds like islands," she remarked pensively.

The governess coughed.

" Majora, Minora, Alderney, and Sark," explained her pupil.

I looked at her severely.

" If you are not careful, April," I said, " you'll be a genius when you grow up and disgrace your parents."

Miss Jones looked as though she did not like Germans. I am afraid she despises us because she thinks we are foreigners—an attitude of mind quite British and wholly to her credit ; but we, on the other hand, regard *her* as a foreigner, which, of course, makes things very complicated.

" Shall I really have to have this strange girl ? " I asked, addressing nobody in particular and not expecting a reply.

" You need not have her," said the Man of Wrath composedly, " but you will. You will write to-day and cordially invite her, and when she has been here twenty-four hours you will quarrel with her. I know you, my dear."

" Quarrel ! I ? With a little art-student ? "

Miss Jones cast down her eyes. She is perpetually scenting a scene, and is always ready to bring whole batteries of discretion and tact and good taste to bear on us, and seems to know we are disputing in an unseemly manner when we would never dream it ourselves but for the warning of her downcast eyes. I would take my courage in both hands and ask her to go, for besides this superfluity of discreet behaviour she is, although only nursery, much too zealous, and inclined to be always teaching and never playing ; but, un-fortunately, the April baby adores her and is sure there never was any one so beautiful before. She comes every day with fresh accounts of the splendours of her wardrobe, and feeling descriptions of her umbrellas and hats ; and Miss Jones looks offended and purses up her lips. In common with most governesses she has a little dark down on her upper lip, and the April baby appeared one day at dinner with her own decorated in faithful imitation, having achieved it after much struggling, with the aid of a lead pencil and unbounded love. Miss Jones put her in the corner for impertinence. I wonder why governesses are so unpleasant. The Man of Wrath says it is because they are not married. Without venturing to differ entirely from the opinion of experience, I would add that the strain of continually having to set an example must surely be very great. It is much easier, and often more pleasant, to be a warning than an example, and governesses are but women, and women are sometimes foolish, and when you want to be foolish it must be annoying to have to be wise.

Minora and Irais arrived yesterday together; or rather, when the carriage drove up, Irais got out of it alone, and informed me that there was a strange girl on a bicycle a little way behind. I sent back the carriage to pick her up, for it was dusk and the roads are terrible.

" But why do you have strange girls here at all ?" asked Irais rather peevishly, taking off her hat in the library before the fire, and otherwise making herself very much at home ; " I don't like them. I'm not sure that they're not worse than husbands who are out of order. Who is she ? She would bicycle from the station, and is, I am sure, the first woman who has done it. The little boys threw stones at her."

" Oh, my dear, that only shows the ignorance of the little boys. Never mind her. Let us have tea in peace before she comes."

" But we should be much happier without her," she grumbled. " Weren't we happy enough in the summer, Elizabeth—just you and I ? "

" Yes, indeed we were," I answered heartily, putting my arms round her. The flame of my affection for Irais burns very brightly on the day of her arrival ; besides, this time I have prudently provided against her sinning with the salt-cellars by ordering them to be handed round like vegetable dishes. We had finished tea and she had gone up to her room to dress before Minora and her bicycle were got here. I hurried out to meet her, feeling sorry for her, plunged into a circle of strangers at such a very personal season as Christmas. But she was not very shy; indeed, she was less shy than I was, and lingered in the hall, giving the servants directions to wipe the snow off the tyres of her machine before she lent an attentive ear to my welcoming remarks.

" I couldn't make your man understand me at the station," she said at last, when her mind was at rest about her bicycle ; " I asked him how far it was, and what the roads were like, and he only smiled. Is he German ? But of course he is — how odd that he didn't understand. You speak English very well, — very well indeed, do you know."

By this time we were in the library, and she stood on the hearth-rug warming her back while I poured her out some tea.

" What a quaint room," she remarked, looking round, " and the hall is so curious too. Very old, isn't it ? There's a lot of copy here."

The Man of Wrath, who had been in the hall on her arrival and had come in with us, began to look about on the carpet. "Copy?" he inquired, " Where's copy ? "

" Oh—material, you know, for a book. I'm just jotting down what strikes me in your country, and when I have time shall throw it into book form." She spoke very loud, as English people always do to foreigners.

" My dear," I said breathlessly to Irais, when I had got into her room and shut the door and Minora was safely in hers, " what do you think—she writes books ! "

" What—the bicycling girl ? "

" Yes—Minora—imagine it ! "

We stood and looked at each other with awe-struck faces.

" How dreadful ! " murmured Irais. " I never met a young girl who did that before."

" She says this place is full of copy."

" Full of what ? "

" That's what you make books with."

" Oh, my dear, this is worse than I

expected ! A strange girl is always a bore
among good friends, but one can generally
manage her. But a girl who writes books—
why, it isn't respectable ! And you can't
snub that sort of people ; they're un-
snubbable."

" Oh, but we'll try ! " I cried, with such
heartiness that we both laughed.

The hall and the library struck Minora
most ; indeed, she lingered so long after
dinner in the hall, which is cold, that the
Man of Wrath put on his fur coat by way
of a gentle hint. His hints are always
gentle.

She wanted to hear the whole story about
the chapel and the nuns and Gustavus
Adolphus, and pulling out a fat note-book
began to take down what I said. I at once
relapsed into silence.

" Well ? " she said.

" That's all."

" Oh, but you've only just begun."

" It doesn't go any further. Won't you
come into the library ? "

In the library she again took up her stand

before the fire and warmed herself, and we
sat in a row and were cold. She has a
wonderfully good profile, which is irritating.
The wind, however, is tempered to the shorn
lamb by her eyes being set too closely
together.

Irais lit a cigarette, and leaning back in
her chair, contemplated her critically be-
neath her long eyelashes. " You are writing
a book ? " she asked presently.

" Well—yes, I suppose I may say that I
am. Just my impressions, you know, of
your country. Anything that strikes me
as curious or amusing—I jot it down, and
when I have time shall work it up into
something, I daresay."

" Are you not studying painting ? "

" Yes, but I can't study that for ever.
We have an English proverb : ' Life is short
and Art is long '—too long, I sometimes
think—and writing is a great relaxation
when I am tired."

" What shall you call it ? "

" Oh, I thought of calling it *Journeyings
in Germany*. It sounds well, and would be

correct.   Or *Jottings from German Journey-ings*,—I haven't quite decided yet which."

"By the author of *Prowls in Pomerania*, you might add," suggested Irais.

"And *Drivel from Dresden*," said I.

"And *Bosh from Berlin*," added Irais.

Minora stared.   "I don't think those two last ones would do," she said, "because it is not to be a facetious book.   But your first one is rather a good title," she added, looking at Irais and drawing out her note-book.   "I think I'll just jot that down."

"If you jot down all we say and then publish it, will it still be your book?" asked Irais.

But Minora was so busy scribbling that she did not hear.

"And have *you* no suggestions to make, Sage?" asked Irais, turning to the Man of Wrath, who was blowing out clouds of smoke in silence.

"Oh, do you call him Sage?" cried Minora; "and always in English?"

Irais and I looked at each other.   We knew what we did call him, and were afraid

Minora would in time ferret it out and enter it in her note-book. The Man of Wrath looked none too well pleased to be alluded to under his very nose by our new guest as "him."

"Husbands are always sages," said I gravely.

"Though sages are not always husbands," said Irais with equal gravity. "Sages and husbands — sage and husbands ——" she went on musingly, "what does that remind you of, Miss Minora?"

"Oh, I know,—how stupid of me!" cried Minora eagerly, her pencil in mid-air and her brain clutching at the elusive recollection, "sage and,—why,—yes,—no,—yes, of course — oh," disappointedly, "but that's vulgar—I can't put it in."

"What is vulgar?" I asked.

"She thinks sage and onions is vulgar," said Irais languidly; "but it isn't, it is very good." She got up and walked to the piano, and, sitting down began, after a little wandering over the keys, to sing.

"Do you play?" I asked Minora.

" Yes, but I am afraid I am rather out of practice."

I said no more. I know what *that* sort of playing is.

When we were lighting our bedroom candles Minora began suddenly to speak in an unknown tongue. We stared. " What is the matter with her ?" murmured Irais.

" I thought, perhaps," said Minora in English, " you might prefer to talk German, and as it is all the same to me what I talk——"

" Oh, pray don't trouble," said Irais. " We like airing our English—don't we, Elizabeth ? "

" I don't want my German to get rusty though," said Minora ; " I shouldn't like to forget it."

" Oh, but isn't there an English song," said Irais, twisting round her neck as she preceded us upstairs, " ' 'Tis folly to remember, 'tis wisdom to forget ? ' "

" You are not nervous sleeping alone, I hope," I said hastily.

" What room is she in ? " asked Irais.

" No. 12."

" Oh !—do you believe in ghosts ? "

Minora turned pale.

" What nonsense," said I ; " we have no ghosts here. Good-night. If you want anything, mind you ring."

" And if you see anything curious in that room," called Irais from her bedroom door, " mind you jot it down."

December 27th.—It is the fashion, I believe, to regard Christmas as a bore of rather a gross description, and as a time when you are invited to over-eat yourself, and pretend to be merry without just cause. As a matter of fact, it is one of the prettiest and most poetic institutions possible, if observed in the proper manner, and after having been more or less unpleasant to everybody for a whole year, it is a blessing to be forced on that one day to be amiable, and it is certainly delightful to be able to give presents without being haunted by the conviction that you are spoiling the recipient, and will suffer for it afterwards. Servants are only

big children, and are made just as happy as
children by little presents and nice things to
eat, and, for days beforehand, every time
the three babies go into the garden they
expect to meet the Christ Child with His
arms full of gifts. They firmly believe that
it is thus their presents are brought, and it is
such a charming idea, that Christmas would
be worth celebrating for its sake alone.

As great secrecy is observed, the prepara-
tions devolve entirely on me, and it is not
very easy work, with so many people in our
own house and on each of the farms, and all
the children, big and little, expecting their
share of happiness. The library is unin-
habitable for several days before and after,
as it is there that we have the trees and
presents. All down one side are the trees,
and the other three sides are lined with
tables, a separate one for each person in
the house. When the trees are lighted, and
stand in their radiance shining down on the
happy faces, I forget all the trouble it has
been, and the number of times I have had
to run up and down stairs, and the various

aches in head and feet, and enjoy myself as much as anybody. First the June baby is ushered in, then the others and ourselves according to age, then the servants, then come the head inspector and his family, the other inspectors from the different farms, the mamsells, the book-keepers and secretaries, and then all the children, troops and troops of them—the big ones leading the little ones by the hand and carrying the babies in their arms, and the mothers peeping round the door. As many as can get in stand in front of the trees, and sing two or three carols; then they are given their presents, and go off triumphantly, making room for the next batch. My three babies sang lustily too, whether they happened to know what was being sung or not. They had on white dresses in honour of the occasion, and the June baby was even arrayed in a low-necked and short-sleeved garment, after the manner of Teutonic infants, whatever the state of the thermometer. Her arms are like miniature prizefighter's arms — I never saw such things;

they are the pride and joy of her little nurse, who had tied them up with blue ribbons, and kept on kissing them. I shall certainly not be able to take her to balls when she grows up, if she goes on having arms like that.

When they came to say good-night, they were all very pale and subdued. The April baby had an exhausted-looking Japanese doll with her, which she said she was taking to bed, not because she liked him, but because she was so sorry for him, he seemed so very tired. They kissed me absently, and went away, only the April baby glancing at the trees as she passed and making them a curtsey.

" Good-bye, trees," I heard her say ; and then she made the Japanese doll bow to them, which he did, in a very languid and blasé fashion. " *You'll* never see such trees again," she told him, giving him a vindictive shake, " for you'll be brokened *long* before next time."

She went out, but came back as though she had forgotten something.

" Thank the *Christkind* so *much*, Mummy, won't you, for all the lovely things He brought us. I suppose you're writing to Him now, isn't you ? "

I cannot see that there was anything gross about our Christmas, and we were perfectly merry without any need to pretend, and for at least two days it brought us a little nearer together, and made us kind. Happiness is so wholesome ; it invigorates and warms me into piety far more effectually than any amount of trials and griefs, and an unexpected pleasure is the surest means of bringing me to my knees. In spite of the protestations of some peculiarly constructed persons that they are the better for trials, I don't believe it. Such things must sour us, just as happiness must sweeten us, and make us kinder, and more gentle. And will anybody affirm that it behoves us to be more thankful for trials than for blessings ? We were meant to be happy, and to accept all the happiness offered with thankfulness— indeed, we are none of us ever thankful enough, and yet we each get so much, so very much, more than we deserve. I know a woman—she stayed with me last summer—who rejoices grimly when those she loves suffer. She believes that it is our lot, and that it braces us and does us good, and she would shield no one from even unnecessary pain; she weeps with the sufferer, but is convinced it is all for the best. Well, let her continue in her dreary beliefs; she has no garden to teach her the beauty and the happiness of holiness, nor does she in the least desire to possess one; her convictions have the sad gray colouring of the dingy streets and houses she lives amongst—the sad colour of humanity in masses. Submission to what people call their "lot" is simply ignoble. If your lot makes you cry and be wretched, get rid of it and take another; strike out for yourself; don't listen to the shrieks of your relations, to their gibes or their entreaties; don't let your own microscopic set prescribe your goings-out and comings-in; don't be afraid of public opinion in the shape of the neighbour in the next house, when all the world is before you new and shining, and everything is possible, if you will only be energetic and independent and seize opportunity by the scruff of the neck.

" To hear you talk," said Irais, " no one would ever imagine that you dream away your days in a garden with a book, and that you never in your life seized anything by the scruff of its neck. And what is scruff ? I hope I have not got any on me." And she craned her neck before the glass.

She and Minora were going to help me decorate the trees, but very soon Irais wandered off to the piano, and Minora was tired and took up a book ; so I called in Miss Jones and the babies,—it was Miss Jones's last public appearance, as I shall relate— and after working for the best part of two days they were finished, and looked like lovely ladies in widespreading, sparkling petticoats, holding up their skirts with glittering fingers. Minora wrote a long description of them for a chapter of her book which is headed *Noel*,—I saw that much, because she left it open on the table while she went to talk to Miss Jones. They were fast friends from the very first, and though it is said to be natural to take to one's own countrymen, I am unable altogether to sympathise with such a reason for sudden affection.

" I wonder what they talk about ? " I said to Irais yesterday, when there was no getting Minora to come to tea, so deeply was she engaged in conversation with Miss Jones.

" Oh, my dear, how can I tell ? Lovers, I suppose, or else they think they are clever and then they talk rubbish."

" Well, of course, Minora thinks she is clever."

" I suppose she does. What does it matter what she thinks ? Why does your governess look so gloomy ? When I see her at luncheon I always imagine she must have just heard that somebody is dead. But she can't hear that every day. What is the matter with her ? "

" I don't think she feels quite as proper as she looks," I said doubtfully ; I was for ever trying to account for Miss Jones's expression.

" But that must be rather nice," said Irais. " It would be awful for her if she felt exactly the same as she looks."

At that moment the door leading into the schoolroom opened softly, and the April baby, tired of playing, came in and sat down at my feet, leaving the door open ; and this is what we heard Miss Jones saying—

" Parents are seldom wise, and the strain the conscientious place upon themselves to appear so before their children and governess must be terrible. Nor are clergymen more pious than other men, yet they have continually to pose before their flock as such. As for governesses, Miss Minora, I know what I am saying when I affirm that there is nothing more intolerable than to have to be polite, and even humble, to persons whose weaknesses and follies are glaringly apparent in every word they utter, and to be forced by the presence of children and employers to a dignity of manner in no way corresponding to one's feelings. The grave father of a family, who was probably one of the least respectable of bachelors, is an interesting study at his own table, where he is constrained to assume airs of infallibility merely because his children are looking at him. The fact of his being a parent does not endow him with any supreme and sudden virtue ; and I can assure you that among the eyes fixed upon him, not the least critical and amused are those of the humble person who fills the post of governess."

" Oh, Miss Jones, how lovely ! " we heard Minora say in accents of rapture, while we sat transfixed with horror at these sentiments. " Do you mind if I put that down in my book ? You say it all so beautifully."

" Without a few hours of relaxation," continued Miss Jones, " of private indemnification for the toilsome virtues displayed in public, who could wade through days of correct behaviour ? There would be no reaction, no room for better impulses, no place for repentance. Parents, priests, and governesses would be in the situation of a stout lady who never has a quiet moment in which she can take off her corsets."

" My dear, what a firebrand ! " whispered Irais.

I got up and went in. They were sitting on the sofa, Minora with clasped hands, gazing admiringly into Miss Jones's face, which wore a very different expression from the one of sour and unwilling propriety I have been used to seeing.

" May I ask you to come to tea ? " I said to Minora. " And I should like to have the children a little while."

She got up very reluctantly, but I waited with the door open until she had gone in and the two babies had followed. They had been playing at stuffing each other's ears with pieces of newspaper while Miss Jones provided Minora with noble thoughts for her work, and had to be tortured afterwards with tweezers. I said nothing to Minora, but kept her with us till dinner-time, and this morning we went for a long sleigh-drive. When we came in to lunch there was no Miss Jones.

" Is Miss Jones ill ? " asked Minora.

" She is gone," I said.

" Gone ? "

" Did you never hear of such things as sick mothers ? " asked Irais blandly ; and we talked resolutely of something else.

All the afternoon Minora has moped. She had found a kindred spirit, and it has been ruthlessly torn from her arms as kindred spirits so often are. It is enough to make her mope, and it is not her fault, poor thing, that she should have preferred the society of a Miss Jones to that of Irais and myself.

At dinner Irais surveyed her with her head on one side. " You look so pale," she said ; " are you not well ? "

Minora raised her eyes heavily, with the patient air of one who likes to be thought a sufferer. " I have a slight headache," she replied gently.

" I hope you are not going to be ill," said Irais with great concern, " because there is only a cow-doctor to be had here, and though he means well, I believe he is rather rough."

Minora was plainly startled. "But what do you do if you are ill ? " she asked.

"Oh, we are never ill," said I ; "the very knowledge that there would be no one to cure us seems to keep us healthy."

"And if any one takes to her bed," said Irais, "Elizabeth always calls in the cow-doctor."

Minora was silent. She feels, I am sure, that she has got into a part of the world peopled solely by barbarians, and that the only civilised creature besides herself has departed and left her at our mercy. Whatever her reflections may be her symptoms are visibly abating.

January 1st.—The service on New Year's Eve is the only one in the whole year that in the least impresses me in our little church, and then the very bareness and ugliness of the place and the ceremonial produce an effect that a snug service in a well-lit church never would. Last night we took Irais and Minora, and drove the three lonely miles in a sleigh. It was pitch - dark, and blowing great guns. We sat wrapped up to our eyes in furs, and as mute as a funeral procession.

" We are going to the burial of our last year's sins," said Irais, as we started ; and there certainly was a funereal sort of feeling in the air. Up in our gallery pew we tried to decipher our chorales by the light of the spluttering tallow candles stuck in holes in the woodwork, the flames wildly blown about by the draughts. The wind banged against the windows in great gusts, screaming louder than the organ, and threatening to blow out the agitated lights altogether. The parson in his gloomy pulpit, surrounded by a frame-work of dusty carved angels, took on an awful appearance of menacing Authority as he raised his voice to make himself heard above the clatter. Sitting there in the dark, I felt very small, and solitary, and defence-less, alone in a great, big, black world. The church was as cold as a tomb ; some of the candles guttered and went out ; the parson in his black robe spoke of death and judg-ment ; I thought I heard a child's voice screaming, and could hardly believe it was only the wind, and felt uneasy and full of forebodings ; all my faith and philosophy deserted me, and I had a horrid feeling that I should probably be well punished, though for what I had no precise idea. If it had not been so dark, and if the wind had not howled so despairingly, I should have paid little attention to the threats issuing from the pulpit ; but, as it was, I fell to making good resolutions. This is always a bad sign, —only those who break them make them ; and if you simply do as a matter of course that which is right as it comes, any preparatory resolving to do so becomes completely superfluous. I have for some years past left off making them on New Year's Eve, and only the gale happening as it did reduced me to doing so last night ; for I have long since discovered that, though the year and the resolutions may be new, I myself am not, and it is worse than useless putting new wine into old bottles.

" But I am not an old bottle," said Irais indignantly, when I held forth to her to the above effect a few hours later in the library, restored to all my philosophy by the warmth and light, " and I find my resolutions carry me very nicely into the spring. I revise them at the end of each month, and strike out the unnecessary ones. By the end of April they have been so severely revised that there are none left."

" There, you see I am right ; if you were not an old bottle your new contents would gradually arrange themselves amiably as a part of you, and the practice of your resolutions would lose its bitterness by becoming a habit."

She shook her head. " Such things never lose their bitterness," she said, " and that is why I don't let them cling to me right into the summer. When May comes, I give myself up to jollity with all the rest of the world, and am too busy being happy to bother about anything I may have resolved when the days were cold and dark."

" And that is just why I love you," I thought. She often says what I feel.

" I wonder," she went on after a pause, " whether men ever make resolutions ? "

" I don't think they do. Only women indulge in such luxuries. It is a nice sort of
feeling, when you have nothing else to do,
giving way to endless grief and penitence,
and steeping yourself to the eyes in con-
trition ; but it is silly. Why cry over things
that are done ? Why do naughty things at
all, if you are going to repent afterwards ?
Nobody is naughty unless they like being
naughty ; and nobody ever really repents
unless they are afraid they are going to be
found out."

" By ' nobody ' of course you mean
women," said Irais.

" Naturally ; the terms are synonymous.
Besides, men generally have the courage of
their opinions."

" I hope you are listening, Miss Minora,"
said Irais in the amiably polite tone she
assumes whenever she speaks to that young
person.

It was getting on towards midnight, and
we were sitting round the fire, waiting for
the New Year, and sipping *Glühwein*, prepared at a small table by the Man of Wrath.

It was hot, and sweet, and rather nasty, but it is proper to drink it on this one night, so of course we did.

Minora does not like either Irais or myself. We very soon discovered that, and laugh about it when we are alone together. I can understand her disliking Irais, but she must be a perverse creature not to like me. Irais has poked fun at her, and I have been, I hope, very kind; yet we are bracketed together in her black books. It is also apparent that she looks upon the Man of Wrath as an interesting example of an ill-used and misunderstood husband, and she is disposed to take him under her wing, and defend him on all occasions against us. He never speaks to her; he is at all times a man of few words, but, as far as Minora is concerned, he might have no tongue at all, and sits sphinx-like and impenetrable while she takes us to task about some remark of a profane nature that we may have addressed to him. One night, some days after her arrival, she developed a skittishness of manner which has since disappeared, and tried to be playful with him;

but you might as well try to be playful with a graven image. The wife of one of the servants had just produced a boy, the first after a series of five daughters, and at dinner we drank the health of all parties concerned, the Man of Wrath making the happy father drink a glass off at one gulp, his heels well together in military fashion. Minora thought the incident typical of German manners, and not only made notes about it, but joined heartily in the health-drinking, and afterwards grew skittish.

She proposed, first of all, to teach us a dance called, I think, the Washington Post, and which was, she said, much danced in England ; and, to induce us to learn, she played the tune to us on the piano. We remained untouched by its beauties, each buried in an easy-chair toasting our toes at the fire. Amongst those toes were those of the Man of Wrath who sat peaceably reading a book and smoking. Minora volunteered to show us the steps, and as we still did not move, danced solitary behind our chairs. Irais did not even turn

her head to look, and I was the only one
amiable or polite enough to do so. Do I
deserve to be placed in Minora's list of disagreeable people side by side with Irais ?
Certainly not. Yet I most surely am.

" It wants the music, of course," observed
Minora breathlessly, darting in and out
between the chairs, apparently addressing
me, but glancing at the Man of Wrath.

No answer from anybody.

" It is *such* a pretty dance," she panted
again, after a few more gyrations.

No answer.

" And is all the rage at home."

No answer.

" Do let me teach you. Won't *you* try,
Herr Sage ? "

She went up to him and dropped him
a little curtsey. It is thus she always
addresses him, entirely oblivious to the
fact, so patent to every one else, that
he resents it.

" Oh come, put away that tiresome old
book," she went on gaily, as he did not
move ; " I am certain it is only some dry

agricultural work that you just nod over. Dancing is much better for you."

Irais and I looked at one another quite frightened. I am sure we both turned pale when the unhappy girl actually laid hold forcibly of his book, and, with a playful little shriek, ran away with it into the next room, hugging it to her bosom and looking back roguishly over her shoulder at him as she ran. There was an awful pause. We hardly dared raise our eyes. Then the Man of Wrath got up slowly, knocked the ashes off the end of his cigar, looked at his watch, and went out at the opposite door into his own rooms, where he stayed for the rest of the evening. She has never, I must say, been skittish since.

" I hope you are listening, Miss Minora," said Irais, " because this sort of conversation is likely to do you good."

" I always listen when people talk sensibly," replied Minora, stirring her grog.

Irais glanced at her with slightly doubtful eyebrows. " Do you agree with our hostess's description of women ? " she asked after a pause.

" As nobodies ?   No, of course I do not."

" Yet she is right.   In the eye of the law we are literally nobodies in our country. Did you know that women are forbidden to go to political meetings here ? "

" Really ? "   Out came the note-book.

" The law expressly forbids the attendance at such meetings of women, children, and idiots."

" Children and idiots—I understand that," said Minora ; " but women — and classed with children and idiots ? "

" Classed with children and idiots," repeated Irais, gravely nodding her head. " Did you know that the law forbids females of any age to ride on the top of omnibuses or tramcars ? "

" Not really ? "

" Do you know why ? "

" I can't imagine."

" Because in going up and down the stairs those inside might perhaps catch a glimpse of the stocking covering their ankles."

" But what——"

" Did you know that the morals of the German public are in such a shaky condition that a glimpse of that sort would be fatal to them ? "

" But I don't see how a stocking——"

" With stripes round it," said Irais.

" And darns in it," I added.

" —could possibly be pernicious ? "

" ' The Pernicious Stocking ; or, Thoughts on the Ethics of Petticoats,' " said Irais. " Put that down as the name of your next book on Germany."

" I never know," complained Minora, letting her note-book fall, " whether you are in earnest or not."

" Don't you ? " said Irais sweetly.

" Is it true," appealed Minora to the Man of Wrath, busy with his lemons in the background, " that your law classes women with children and idiots ? "

" Certainly," he answered promptly, " and a very proper classification too."

We all looked blank. " That's rude," said I at last.

" Truth is always rude, my dear," he replied complacently. Then he added, " If I were commissioned to draw up a new legal code, and had previously enjoyed the privilege, as I have been doing lately, of listening to the conversation of you three young ladies, I should make precisely the same classification."

Even Minora was incensed at this.

" You are telling us in the most unvarnished manner that we are idiots," said Irais.

" Idiots ? No, no, by no means. But children,—nice little agreeable children. I very much like to hear you talk together. It is all so young and fresh what you think and what you believe, and not of the least consequence to any one."

" Not of the least consequence ? " cried Minora. " What we believe is of very great consequence indeed to us."

" Are you jeering at our beliefs ? " inquired Irais sternly.

" Not for worlds. I would not on any account disturb or change your pretty little beliefs. It is your chief charm that you always believe everything. How desperate would our case be if young ladies only believed facts, and never accepted another person's assurance, but preferred the evidence of their own eyes ! They would have no illusions, and a woman without illusions is the dreariest and most difficult thing to manage possible."

" Thing ? " protested Irais.

The Man of Wrath, usually so silent, makes up for it from time to time by holding forth at unnecessary length. He took up his stand now with his back to the fire, and a glass of *Glühwein* in his hand. Minora had hardly heard his voice before, so quiet has he been since she came, and sat with her pencil raised, ready to fix for ever the wisdom that should flow from his lips.

" What would become of poetry if women became so sensible that they turned a deaf ear to the poetic platitudes of love ? That love does indulge in platitudes I suppose you will admit." He looked at Irais.

" Yes, they all say exactly the same thing," she acknowledged.

" Who could murmur pretty speeches on the beauty of a common sacrifice, if the listener's want of imagination was such as to enable her only to distinguish one victim in the picture, and that one herself ? "

Minora took that down word for word,— much good may it do her.

" Who would be brave enough to affirm that if refused he will die, if his assurances merely elicit a recommendation to diet himself, and take plenty of outdoor exercise ? Women are responsible for such lies, because they believe them. Their amazing vanity makes them swallow flattery so gross that it is an insult, and men will always be ready to tell the precise number of lies that a woman is ready to listen to. Who indulges more recklessly in glowing exaggerations than the lover who hopes, and has not yet obtained ? He will, like the nightingale, sing with unceasing modulations, display all his talent, untiringly repeat his sweetest notes, until he has what he wants, when his song, like the nightingale's, immediately ceases, never again to be heard."

"Take that down," murmured Irais aside to Minora — unnecessary advice, for her pencil was scribbling as fast as it could.

"A woman's vanity is so immeasurable that, after having had ninety-nine object-lessons in the difference between promise and performance and the emptiness of pretty speeches, the beginning of the hundredth will find her lending the same willing and enchanted ear to the eloquence of flattery as she did on the occasion of the first. What can the exhortations of the strong-minded sister, who has never had these experiences, do for such a woman ? It is useless to tell her she is man's victim, that she is his plaything, that she is cheated, down-trodden, kept under, laughed at, shabbily treated in every way—that is not a true statement of the case. She is simply the victim of her own vanity, and against that, against the belief in her own fascinations, against the very part of herself that gives all the colour to her life, who shall expect a woman to take up arms ? "

" Are you so vain, Elizabeth ? " inquired Irais with a shocked face, " and had you lent a willing ear to the blandishments of ninety-nine before you reached your final destiny ? "

" I am one of the sensible ones, I suppose," I replied, " for nobody ever wanted me to listen to blandishments."

Minora sighed.

" I like to hear you talk together about the position of women," he went on, " and wonder when you will realise that they hold exactly the position they are fitted for. As soon as they are fit to occupy a better, no power on earth will be able to keep them out of it. Meanwhile, let me warn you that, as things now are, only strong-minded women wish to see you the equals of men, and the strong-minded are invariably plain. The pretty ones would rather see men their slaves than their equals."

" You know," said Irais, frowning, " that I consider myself strong-minded."

" And never rise till lunch-time ? "

Irais blushed. Although I don't approve of such conduct, it is very convenient in more ways than one ; I get through my housekeeping undisturbed, and, whenever she is disposed to lecture me, I begin about this habit of hers. Her conscience must be terribly stricken on the point, for she is by no means as a rule given to meekness.

" A woman without vanity would be un-attackable," resumed the Man of Wrath. " When a girl enters that downward path that leads to ruin, she is led solely by her own vanity ; for in these days of policemen no young woman can be forced against her will from the path of virtue, and the cries of the injured are never heard until the destroyer begins to express his penitence for having destroyed. If his passion could remain at white-heat and he could continue to feed her ear with the protestations she loves, no principles of piety or virtue would disturb the happiness of his companion ; for a mournful experience teaches that piety begins only where passion ends, and that principles are strongest where temptations are most rare."

" But what has all this to do with us ? " I inquired severely.

" You were displeased at our law classing you as it does, and I merely wish to justify it," he answered. " Creatures who habitually say *yes* to everything a man proposes, when no one can oblige them to say it, and when it is so often fatal, are plainly not responsible beings."

" I shall never say it to you again, my dear man," I said.

" And not only *that* fatal weakness," he continued, " but what is there, candidly, to distinguish you from children ? You are older, but not wiser,—really not so wise, for with years you lose the common sense you had as children. Have you ever heard a group of women talking reasonably together ? "

" Yes—we do ! " Irais and I cried in a breath.

" It has interested me," went on the Man of Wrath, " in my idle moments, to listen

to their talk. It amused me to hear the
malicious little stories they told of their
best friends who were absent, to note the
spiteful little digs they gave their best
friends who were present, to watch the utter
incredulity with which they listened to the
tale of some other woman's conquests, the
radiant good faith they displayed in connec-
tion with their own, the instant collapse
into boredom, if some topic of so - called
general interest, by some extraordinary
chance, were introduced."

" You must have belonged to a particularly nice set," remarked Irais.

" And as for politics," he said, " I have
never heard them mentioned among women."

" Children and idiots are not interested in
such things," I said.

" And we are much too frightened of being
put in prison," said Irais.

" In prison ? " echoed Minora.

" Don't you know," said Irais, turning to
her, " that if you talk about such things
here you run a great risk of being imprisoned ? "

" But why ? "

" But why ? Because, though you yourself may have meant nothing but what was
innocent, your words may have suggested
something less innocent to the evil minds
of your hearers ; and then the law steps in,
and calls it *dolus eventualis,* and everybody
says how dreadful, and off you go to prison
and are punished as you deserve to be."

Minora looked mystified.

" That is not, however, your real reason
for not discussing them," said the Man of
Wrath ; " they simply do not interest you.
Or it may be, that you do not consider your
female friends' opinions worth listening to,
for you certainly display an astonishing
thirst for information when male politicians
are present. I have seen a pretty young
woman, hardly in her twenties, sitting a
whole evening drinking in the doubtful
wisdom of an elderly political star, with
every appearance of eager interest. He was
a bimetallic star, and was giving her whole
pamphletsful of information."

" She wanted to make up to him for some

reason," said Irais, "and got him to explain his hobby to her, and he was silly enough to be taken in. Now which was the sillier in that case ? "

She threw herself back in her chair and looked up defiantly, beating her foot impatiently on the carpet.

" She wanted to be thought clever," said the Man of Wrath. " What puzzled me," he went on musingly, " was that she went away apparently as serene and happy as when she came. The explanation of the principles of bimetallism produce, as a rule, a contrary effect."

" Why, she hadn't been listening," cried Irais, "and your simple star had been making a fine goose of himself the whole evening.

> " Prattle, prattle, simple star,
> Bimetallic, *wunderbar*.
> Though you're given to describe
> Woman as a *dummes Weib*,
> You yourself are sillier far,
> Prattling, bimetallic star ! "

" No doubt she had understood very little," said the Man of Wrath, taking no notice of this effusion.

" And no doubt the gentleman hadn't understood much either." Irais was plainly irritated.

" Your opinion of woman," said Minora in a very small voice, " is not a high one. But, in the sick chamber, I suppose you agree that no one could take her place ? "

" If you are thinking of hospital-nurses," I said, " I must tell you that I believe he married chiefly that he might have a wife instead of a strange woman to nurse him when he is sick."

" But," said Minora, bewildered at the way her illusions were being knocked about, " the sick-room is surely the very place of all others in which a woman's gentleness and tact are most valuable."

" Gentleness and tact ? " repeated the Man of Wrath. " I have never met those qualities in the professional nurse. According to my experience, she is a disagreeable person who finds in private nursing exquisite opportunities for asserting her superiority over ordinary and prostrate mankind. I know of no more humiliating position for a

man than to be in bed having his feverish
brow soothed by a sprucely-dressed strange
woman, bristling with starch and spotlessness. He would give half his income for
his clothes, and probably the other half if
she would leave him alone, and go away
altogether. He feels her superiority through
every pore ; he never before realised how
absolutely inferior he is ; he is abjectly
polite, and contemptibly conciliatory ; if a
friend comes to see him, he eagerly praises
her in case she should be listening behind
the screen ; he cannot call his soul his own,
and, what is far more intolerable, neither is
he sure that his body really belongs to him ;
he has read of ministering angels and the
light touch of a woman's hand, but the day
on which he can ring for his servant and
put on his socks in private fills him with the
same sort of wildness of joy that he felt as
a home-sick schoolboy at the end of his first
term."

Minora was silent. Irais's foot was livelier
than ever. The Man of Wrath stood smiling
blandly down upon us. You can't argue

with a person so utterly convinced of his
infallibility that he won't even get angry
with you; so we sat round and said
nothing.

"If," he went on, addressing Irais, who
looked rebellious, "you doubt the truth of
my remarks, and still cling to the old poetic
notion of noble, self-sacrificing women tenderly helping the patient over the rough
places on the road to death or recovery, let
me beg you to try for yourself, next time
any one in your house is ill, whether the
actual fact in any way corresponds to the
picturesque belief. The angel who is to
alleviate our sufferings comes in such a
questionable shape, that to the unimagina-
tive she appears merely as an extremely self-
confident young woman, wisely concerned
first of all in securing her personal comfort,
much given to complaints about her food
and to helplessness where she should be
helpful, possessing an extraordinary capacity
for fancying herself slighted, or not regarded
as the superior being she knows herself to
be, morbidly anxious lest the servants should,

by some mistake, treat her with offensive cordiality, pettish if the patient gives more trouble than she had expected, intensely injured and disagreeable if he is made so courageous by his wretchedness as to wake her during the night—an act of desperation of which I was guilty once, and once only. Oh, these good women! What sane man wants to have to do with angels? And especially do we object to having them about us when we are sick and sorry, when we feel in every fibre what poor things we are, and when all our fortitude is needed to enable us to bear our temporary inferiority patiently, without being forced besides to assume an attitude of eager and grovelling politeness towards the angel in the house."

There was a pause.

"I didn't know you could talk so much, Sage," said Irais at length.

"What would you have women do, then?" asked Minora meekly. Irais began to beat her foot up and down again,—what did it matter what Men of Wrath would have us do? "There are not," continued Minora, blushing, " husbands enough for every one, and the rest must do something."

" Certainly," replied the oracle. " Study the art of pleasing by dress and manner as long as you are of an age to interest us, and above all, let all women, pretty and plain, married and single, study the art of cookery. If you are an artist in the kitchen you will always be esteemed."

I sat very still. Every German woman, even the wayward Irais, has learned to cook; I seem to have been the only one who was naughty and wouldn't.

" Only be careful," he went on, " in studying both arts, never to forget the great truth that dinner precedes blandishments and not blandishments dinner. A man must be made comfortable before he will make love to you ; and though it is true that if you offered him a choice between *Spickgans* and kisses, he would say he would take both, yet he would invariably begin with the *Spickgans*, and allow the kisses to wait."

At this I got up, and Irais followed my

example. "Your cynicism is disgusting," I said icily.

"You two are always exceptions to anything I may say," he said, smiling amiably.

He stooped and kissed Irais's hand. She is inordinately vain of her hands, and says her husband married her for their sake, which I can quite believe. I am glad they are on her and not on Minora, for if Minora had had them I should have been annoyed. Minora's are bony, with chilly-looking knuckles, ignored nails, and too much wrist. I feel very well disposed towards her when my eye falls on them. She put one forward now, evidently thinking it would be kissed too.

"Did you know," said Irais, seeing the movement, "that it is the custom here to kiss women's hands?"

"But only married women's," I added, not desiring her to feel out of it, "never young girls'."

She drew it in again. "It is a pretty custom," she said with a sigh; and pensively inscribed it in her book.

January 15*th.*—The bills for my roses and bulbs and other last year's horticultural indulgences were all on the table when I came down to breakfast this morning. They rather frightened me. Gardening is expensive, I find, when it has to be paid for out of one's own private pin-money. The Man of Wrath does not in the least want roses, or flowering shrubs, or plantations, or new paths, and therefore, he asks, why should he pay for them ? So he does not and I do, and I have to make up for it by not indulging all too riotously in new clothes, which is no doubt very chastening. I certainly prefer buying new rose-trees to new dresses, if I cannot comfortably have both ; and I see a time coming when the passion for my garden will have taken such a hold on me that I shall not only entirely cease buying more clothes, but begin to sell those that I already have. The garden is so big that everything has to be bought wholesale ; and I fear I shall not be able to go on much longer with only one man and a stork, because the more I plant the more there will be to water in the inevitable drought, and the watering is a serious consideration when it means going backwards and forwards all day long to a pump near the house, with a little water-cart. People living in England, in almost perpetual mildness and moisture, don't really know what a drought is. If they have some weeks of cloudless weather, it is generally preceded and followed by good rains; but we have perhaps an hour's shower every week, and then comes a month or six weeks' drought. The soil is very light, and dries so quickly that, after the heaviest thunder-shower, I can walk over any of my paths in my thin shoes; and to keep the garden even moderately damp it should pour with rain regularly every day for three hours. My only means of getting water is to go to the pump near the house, or to the little stream that forms my eastern boundary, and the little stream dries up too unless there has been rain, and is at the best of times difficult to get at, having steep banks covered with forget-me-nots. I possess one moist, peaty bit of ground, and that is to

be planted with silver birches in imitation
of the Hirschwald, and is to be carpeted
between the birches with flaming azaleas.
All the rest of my soil is sandy—the soil for
pines and acacias, but not the soil for roses;
yet see what love will do—there are more
roses in my garden than any other flower!
Next spring the bare places are to be filled
with trees that I have ordered: pines behind
the delicate acacias and startling mountain-
ashes, oaks, copper beeches, maples, larches,
juniper-trees — was it not Elijah who sat
down to rest under a juniper tree? I have
often wondered how he managed to get under
it. It is a compact little tree, not more than
two to three yards high here, and all closely
squeezed up together. Perhaps they grew
more aggressively where he was. By the
time the babies have grown old and disagreeable it will be very pretty here, and
then possibly they won't like it; and, if they
have inherited the Man of Wrath's indifference to gardens, they will let it run wild and
leave it to return to the state in which I
found it. Or perhaps their three husbands

will refuse to live in it, or to come to such a
lonely place at all, and then of course its fate
is sealed.   My only comfort is that husbands
don't flourish in the desert, and that the
three will have to wait a long time before
enough are found to go round.   Mothers tell
me that it is a dreadful business finding one
husband ; how much more painful then to
have to look for three at once !—the babies
are so nearly the same age that they only
just escaped being twins.   But I won't look.
I can imagine nothing more uncomfortable
than a son-in-law, and besides, I don't think
a husband is at all a good thing for a girl to
have.   I shall do my best in the years at
my disposal to train them so to love the
garden, and outdoor life, and even farming,
that, if they have a spark of their mother
in them, they will want and ask for nothing
better.   My hope of success is however exceedingly small, and there is probably a
fearful period in store for me when I shall
be taken every day during the winter to the
distant towns to balls—a poor old mother
shivering in broad daylight in her party

gown, and being made to start after an early
lunch and not getting home till breakfast-
time next morning. Indeed, they have
already developed an alarming desire to go
to " partings " as they call them, the April
baby announcing her intention of beginning
to do so when she is twelve. " Are *you*
twelve, Mummy ? " she asked.

The gardener is leaving on the first of
April, and I am trying to find another. It
is grievous changing so often—in two years
I shall have had three — because at each
change a great part of my plants and plans
necessarily suffers. Seeds get lost, seedlings
are not pricked out in time, places already
sown are planted with something else, and
there is confusion out of doors and despair
in my heart. But he was to have married
the cook, and the cook saw a ghost and immediately left, and he is going after. her as
soon as he can, and meanwhile is wasting
visibly away. What she saw was doors
that are locked opening with a great clatter
all by themselves *on the hinge-side*, and then
somebody invisible cursed at her. These

phenomena now go by the name of " the ghost." She asked to be allowed to leave at once, as she had never been in a place where there was a ghost before. I suggested that she should try and get used to it ; but she thought it would be wasting time, and she looked so ill that I let her go, and the garden has to suffer. I don't know why it should be given to cooks to see such interesting things and withheld from me, but I have had two others since she left, and they both have seen the ghost. Minora grows very silent as bed-time approaches, and relents towards Irais and myself; and, after having shown us all day how little she approves us, when the bedroom candles are brought she quite begins to cling. She has once or twice anxiously inquired whether Irais is sure she does not object to sleeping alone.

" If you are at all nervous, I will come and keep you company," she said ; " I don't mind at all, I assure you."

But Irais is not to be taken in by such simple wiles, and has told me she would rather sleep with fifty ghosts than with one Minora.

Since Miss Jones was so unexpectedly called away to her parent's bedside I have seen a good deal of the babies ; and it is so nice without a governess that I would put off engaging another for a year or two, if it were not that I should in so doing come within the reach of the arm of the law, which is what every German spends his life in trying to avoid. The April baby will be six next month, and, after her sixth birthday is passed, we are liable at any moment to receive a visit from a school inspector, who will inquire curiously into the state of her education, and, if it is not up to the required standard, all sorts of fearful things might happen to the guilty parents, probably beginning with fines, and going on *crescendo* to dungeons if, owing to gaps between governesses and difficulties in finding the right one, we persisted in our evil courses. Shades of the prison-house begin to close here upon the growing boy, and prisons compass the Teuton about on every side all through life to such an extent that he has to walk very delicately indeed if he would stay outside them and pay for their maintenance. Cultured individuals do not, as a rule, neglect to teach their offspring to read, and write, and say their prayers, and are apt to resent the intrusion of an examining inspector into their homes; but it does not much matter after all, and I daresay it is very good for us to be worried; indeed, a philosopher of my acquaintance declares that people who are not regularly and properly worried are never any good for anything. In the eye of the law we are all sinners, and every man is held to be guilty until he has proved that he is innocent.

Minora has seen so much of the babies that, after vainly trying to get out of their way for several days, she thought it better to resign herself, and make the best of it by regarding them as copy, and using them to fill a chapter in her book. So she took to dogging their footsteps wherever they went, attended their uprisings and their lyings down, engaged them, if she could, in intelligent conversation, went with them into the garden to study their ways when they were sleighing, drawn by a big dog, and generally made their lives a burden to them. This went on for three days, and then she settled down to write the result with the Man of Wrath's typewriter, borrowed whenever her notes for any chapter have reached the state of ripeness necessary for the process she describes as "throwing into form." She writes everything with a typewriter, even her private letters.

"Don't forget to put in something about a mother's knee," said Irais; "you can't write effectively about children without that."

"Oh, of course I shall mention that," replied Minora.

"And pink toes," I added. "There are always toes, and they are never anything but pink."

"I have that somewhere," said Minora, turning over her notes.

"But, after all, babies are not a German speciality," said Irais, "and I don't quite see why you should bring them into a book of German travels. Elizabeth's babies have each got the fashionable number of arms and legs, and are exactly the same as English ones."

"Oh, but they can't be *just* the same, you know," said Minora, looking worried. "It must make a difference living here in this place, and eating such odd things, and never having a doctor, and never being ill. Children who have never had measles and those things can't be quite the same as other children ; it must all be in their systems and can't get out for some reason or other. And a child brought up on chicken and rice-pudding must be different to a child that eats *Spickgans* and liver sausages. And they *are* different ; I can't tell in what way, but they certainly are ; and I think if I steadily describe them from the materials I have collected the last three days, I may perhaps hit on the points of difference."

"Why bother about points of difference ? " asked Irais. " I should write some little thing, bringing in the usual parts of the picture, such as knees and toes, and make it mildly pathetic."

" But it is by no means an easy thing for me to do," said Minora plaintively ; " I have so little experience of children."

" Then why write it at all ? " asked that sensible person Elizabeth.

" I have as little experience as you," said Irais, " because I have no children ; but if you don't yearn after startling originality, nothing is easier than to write bits about them. I believe I could do a dozen in an hour."

She sat down at the writing-table, took up an old letter, and scribbled for about five minutes. " There," she said, throwing it to Minora, " you may have it—pink toes and all complete."

Minora put on her eye-glasses and read aloud : " When my baby shuts her eyes and sings her hymns at bed-time my stale and battered soul is filled with awe. All sorts of vague memories crowd into my mind— memories of my own mother and myself— how many years ago !—of the sweet help- lessness of being gathered up half asleep in her arms, and undressed, and put in my cot,

without being wakened ; of the angels I believed in ; of little children coming straight
from heaven, and still being surrounded, so
long as they were good, by the shadow of
white wings,—all the dear poetic nonsense
learned, just as my baby is learning it, at
her mother's knee. She has not an idea of
the beauty of the charming things she is
told, and stares wide - eyed, with heavenly
eyes, while her mother talks of the heaven
she has so lately come from, and is relieved
and comforted by the interrupting bread
and milk. At two years old she does not
understand angels, and does understand
bread and milk ; at five she has vague
notions about them, and prefers bread and
milk ; at ten both bread and milk and angels
have been left behind in the nursery, and
she has already found out that they are
luxuries not necessary to her everyday life.
In later years she may be disinclined to
accept truths second-hand, insist on thinking for herself, be earnest in her desire to
shake off exploded traditions, be untiring
in her efforts to live according to a high

moral standard and to be strong, and pure, and good——"

"Like tea," explained Irais.

"—yet will she never, with all her virtues, possess one-thousandth part of the charm that clung about her when she sang, with quiet eyelids, her first reluctant hymns, kneeling on her mother's knees. I love to come in at bed-time and sit in the window in the setting sunshine watching the mysteries of her going to bed. Her mother tubs her, for she is far too precious to be touched by any nurse, and then she is rolled up in a big bath towel, and only her little pink toes peep out; and when she is powdered, and combed, and tied up in her night-dress, and all her curls are on end, and her ears glowing, she is knelt down on her mother's lap, a little bundle of fragrant flesh, and her face reflects the quiet of her mother's face as she goes through her evening prayer for pity and for peace."

"How very curious!" said Minora, when she had finished. "That is exactly what I was going to say."

" Oh, then I have saved you the trouble
of putting it together ; you can copy that
if you like."

" But have you a stale soul, Miss Minora ? "
I asked.

" Well, do you know, I rather think that
is a good touch," she replied ; " it will make
people really think a man wrote the book.
You know I am going to take a man's
name."

" That is precisely what I imagined," said
Irais. " You will call yourself John Jones,
or George Potts, or some such sternly
commonplace name, to emphasise your un-
compromising attitude towards all feminine
weaknesses, and no one will be taken in."

" I really think, Elizabeth," said Irais to
me later, when the click of Minora's typewriter was heard hesitating in the next
room, " that you and I are writing her book
for her. She takes down everything we
say. Why does she copy all that about the
baby ? I wonder why mothers' knees are
supposed to be touching ? I never learned
anything at them, did you ? But then in

my case they were only stepmother's, and nobody ever sings their praises."

" My mother was always at parties," I said ; " and the nurse made me say my prayers in French."

" And as for tubs and powder," went on Irais, " when I was a baby such things were not the fashion. There were never any bathrooms, and no tubs ; our faces and hands were washed, and there was a foot-bath in the room, and in the summer we had a bath and were put to bed afterwards for fear we might catch cold. My step-mother didn't worry much ; she used to wear pink dresses all over lace, and the older she got the prettier the dresses got. When is she going ? "

" Who ? Minora ? I haven't asked her that."

" ·Then I will. It is really bad for her art to be neglected like this. She has been here an unconscionable time,—it must be nearly three weeks."

" Yes, she came the same day you did," I said pleasantly.

Irais was silent.   I hope she was reflecting that it is not worse to neglect one's art than one's husband, and her husband is lying all this time stretched on a bed of sickness, while she is spending her days so agreeably with me.   She has a way of forgetting that she has a home, or any other business in the world than just to stay on chatting with me, and reading, and singing, and laughing at any one there is to laugh at, and kissing the babies, and tilting with the Man of Wrath. Naturally I love her—she is so pretty that anybody with eyes in his head must love her —but too much of anything is bad, and next month the passages and offices are to be whitewashed, and people who have ever whitewashed their houses inside know what nice places they are to live in while it is being done; and there will be no dinner for Irais, and none of those succulent salads full of caraway seeds that she so devotedly loves. I shall begin to lead her thoughts gently back to her duties by inquiring every day anxiously after her husband's health.   She is not very fond of him, because he does not

run and hold the door open for her every
time she gets up to leave the room ; and
though she has asked him to do so, and told
him how much she wishes he would, he still
won't. She stayed once in a house where
there was an Englishman, and his nimble-
ness in regard to doors and chairs so im-
pressed her that her husband has had no
peace since, and each time she has to go out
of a room she is reminded of her disregarded
wishes, so that a shut door is to her sym-
bolic of the failure of her married life, and
the very sight of one makes her wonder why
she was born ; at least, that is what she
told me once, in a burst of confidence. He
is quite a nice, harmless little man, pleasant
to talk to, good-tempered, and full of fun ;
but he thinks he is too old to begin to learn
new and uncomfortable ways, and he has
that horror of being made better by his wife
that distinguishes so many righteous men,
and is shared by the Man of Wrath, who per-
sists in holding his glass in his left hand at
meals, because if he did not (and I don't
believe he particularly likes doing it) his

relations might say that marriage has improved him, and thus drive the iron into his soul. This habit occasions an almost daily argument between one or other of the babies and myself.

" April, hold your glass in your right hand."

" But papa doesn't."

" When you are as old as papa you can do as you like."

This was embellished only yesterday by Minora adding impressively, " And only think how strange it would look if *everybody* held their glasses so."

April was greatly struck by the force of this proposition.

January 28th.—It is very cold,—fifteen degrees of frost *Réaumur*, but perfectly delicious, still, bright weather, and one feels jolly and energetic and amiably disposed towards everybody. The two young ladies are still here, but the air is so buoyant that even they don't weigh on me any longer, and besides, they have both announced their approaching departure, so that after all I shall get my whitewashing done in peace, and the house will have on its clean pinafore in time to welcome the spring.

Minora has painted my portrait, and is going to present it as a parting gift to the Man of Wrath ; and the fact that I let her do it, and sat meekly times innumerable, proves conclusively, I hope, that I am not vain. When Irais first saw it she laughed till she cried, and at once commissioned her to paint hers, so that she may take it away with her and give it to her husband on his birthday, which happens to be early in February. Indeed, if it were not for this birthday, I really think she would have forgotten to go at all ; but birthdays are great and solemn festivals with us, never allowed to slip by unnoticed, and always celebrated in the presence of a sympathetic crowd of relations (gathered from far and near to tell you how well you are wearing, and that nobody would ever dream, and that really it is wonderful), who stand round a sort of sacrificial altar, on which your years

are offered up as a burnt-offering to the gods
in the shape of lighted pink and white
candles, stuck in a very large, flat, jammy
cake. The cake with its candles is the chief
feature, and on the table round it lie the
gifts each person present is more or less
bound to give. As my birthday falls in
the winter I get mittens as well as blotting-
books and photograph-frames, and if it were
in the summer I should get photograph-
frames and blotting-books and no mittens ;
but whatever the present may be, and by
whomsoever given, it has to be welcomed
with the noisiest gratitude, and loudest
exclamations of joy, and such words as
entzückend, reizend, herrlich, wundervoll, and
süss repeated over and over again, until the
unfortunate *Geburtstagskind* feels indeed that
another year has gone, and that she has
grown older, and wiser, and more tired of
folly and of vain repetitions. A flag is
hoisted, and all the morning the rites are
celebrated, the cake eaten, healths drunk,
speeches made, and hands nearly shaken
off. The neighbouring parsons drive up,

and when nobody is looking their wives
count the candles in the cake ; the active
lady in the next *Schloss* spares time to send
a pot of flowers, and to look up my age in
the *Gotha Almanach* ; a deputation comes
from the farms, headed by the chief inspector in white kid gloves who invokes
Heaven's blessings on the gracious lady's
head ; and the babies are enchanted, and
sit in a corner trying on all the mittens. In
the evening there is a dinner for the relations
and the chief local authorities, with more
health-drinking and speechifying, and next
morning, when I come downstairs thankful
to have done with it, I am confronted by
the altar still in its place, cake crumbs and
candle-grease and all, because any hasty
removal of it would imply a most lamentable
want of sentiment, deplorable in anybody,
but scandalous and disgusting in a tender
female. All birthdays are observed in this
fashion, and not a few wise persons go for
a short trip just about the time theirs is due,
and I think I shall imitate them next year ;
only trips to the country or seaside in

December are not usually pleasant, and if I
go to a town there are sure to be relations
in it, and then the cake will spring up
mushroom - like from the teeming soil of
their affection.

I hope it has been made evident in these
pages how superior Irais and myself are
to the ordinary weaknesses of mankind ; if
any further proof were needed, it is furnished
by the fact that we both, in defiance of
tradition, scorn this celebration of birthday
rites. Years ago, when first I knew her, and
long before we were either of us married, I
sent her a little brass candlestick on her
birthday ; and when mine followed a few
months later, she sent me a note-book. No
notes were written in it, and on her next
birthday I presented it to her ; she thanked
me profusely in the customary manner, and
when my turn came I received the brass
candlestick. Since then we alternately enjoy
the possession of each of these articles, and
the present question is comfortably settled
once and for all, at a minimum of trouble
and expense. We never mention this little

arrangement except at the proper time, when we send a letter of fervid thanks.

This radiant weather, when mere living is a joy, and sitting still over the fire out of the question, has been going on for more than a week. Sleighing and skating have been our chief occupation, especially skating, which is more than usually fascinating here, because the place is intersected by small canals communicating with a lake and the river belonging to the lake, and as everything is frozen black and hard, we can skate for miles straight ahead without being obliged to turn round and come back again, —at all times an annoying, and even mortifying, proceeding. Irais skates beautifully; modesty is the only obstacle to my saying the same of myself, but I may remark that all Germans skate well, for the simple reason that every year of their lives, for three or four months, they may do it as much as they like. Minora was astonished and disconcerted by finding herself left behind, and arriving at the place where tea meets us half an hour after we had finished.

In some places the banks of the canals are so high that only our heads appear level with the fields, and it is, as Minora noted in her book, a curious sight to see three female heads skimming along apparently by themselves, and enjoying it tremendously. When the banks are low, we appear to be gliding deliciously over the roughest ploughed fields, with or without legs according to circumstances. Before we start, I fix on the place where tea and a sleigh are to meet us, and we drive home again ; because skating against the wind is as detestable as skating with it is delightful, and an unkind Nature arranges its blowing without the smallest regard for our convenience.

Yesterday, by way of a change, we went for a picnic to the shores of the Baltic, icebound at this season, and utterly desolate at our nearest point. I have a weakness for picnics, especially in winter, when the mosquitoes cease from troubling and the ant-hills are at rest ; and of all my many favourite picnic spots this one on the Baltic is the loveliest and best. As it is a three-hours' drive, the Man of Wrath is loud in his lamentations when the special sort of weather comes which means, as experience has taught him, this particular excursion. There must be deep snow, hard frost, no wind, and a cloudless sky ; and when, on waking up, I see these conditions fulfilled, then it would need some very potent reason to keep me from having out a sleigh and going off. It is, I admit, a hard day for the horses ; but why have horses if they are not to take you where you want to go to, and at the time you want to go ? And why should not horses have hard days as well as everybody else ? The Man of Wrath loathes picnics, and has no eye for nature and frozen seas, and is simply bored by a long drive through a forest that does not belong to him ; a single turnip on his own place is more admirable in his eyes than the tallest, pinkest, straightest pine that ever reared its snow-crowned head against the setting sunlight. Now observe the superiority of woman, who sees that both are good, and after having gazed at the pine and been made happy by its beauty, goes home and placidly eats the turnip. He went once and only once to this particular place, and made us feel so small by his *blasé* behaviour that I never invite him now. It is a beautiful spot, endless forest stretching along the shore as far as the eye can reach ; and after driving through it for miles you come suddenly, at the end of an avenue of arching trees, upon the glistening oily sea, with the orange-coloured sails of distant fishing-smacks shining in the sunlight. Whenever I have been there it has been windless weather, and the silence so profound that I could hear my pulses beating. The humming of insects and the sudden scream of a jay are the only sounds in summer, and in winter the stillness is the stillness of death.

Every paradise has its serpent, however, and this one is so infested by mosquitoes during the season when picnics seem most natural, that those of my visitors who have been taken there for a treat have invariably lost their tempers, and made the quiet shores ring with their wailing and lamentations.

These despicable but irritating insects don't seem to have anything to do but to sit in multitudes on the sand, waiting for any prey Providence may send them; and as soon as the carriage appears they rise up in a cloud, and rush to meet us, almost dragging us out bodily, and never leave us until we drive away again. The sudden view of the sea from the mossy, pine-covered height directly above it where we picnic; the wonderful stretch of lonely shore with the forest to the water's edge; the coloured sails in the blue distance; the freshness, the brightness, the vastness—all is lost upon the picnickers, and made worse than. indifferent to them, by the perpetual necessity they are under of fighting these horrid creatures. It is nice being the only person who ever goes there or shows it to anybody, but if more people went, perhaps the mosquitoes would be less lean, and hungry, and pleased to see us. It has, however, the advantage of being a suitable place to which to take refractory visitors when they have stayed too long, or left my books out in the garden all night, or otherwise made their presence a burden too grievous to be borne ; then one fine hot morning when they are all looking limp, I suddenly propose a picnic on the Baltic. I have never known this proposal fail to be greeted with exclamations of surprise and delight.

"The Baltic ! You never told us you were within driving distance ? How *heavenly* to get a breath of sea air on a day like this ! The very *thought* puts new life into one ! And how *delightful* to see the Baltic ! Oh, *please* take us ! " And then I take them.

But on a brilliant winter's day my conscience is as clear as the frosty air itself, and yesterday morning we started off in the gayest of spirits, even Minora being disposed to laugh immoderately on the least provocation. Only our eyes were allowed to peep out from the fur and woollen wrappings necessary to our heads if we would come back with our ears and noses in the same places they were in when we started, and for the first two miles the mirth created by each other's strange appearance was uproarious,—a fact I mention merely to show what an effect dry, bright, intense cold produces on healthy bodies, and how much better it is to go out in it and enjoy it than to stay indoors and sulk. As we passed through the neighbouring village with cracking of whip and jingling of bells, heads popped up at the windows to stare, and the only living thing in the silent, sunny street was a melancholy fowl with ruffled feathers, which looked at us reproachfully, as we dashed with so much energy over the crackling snow.

" Oh, foolish bird ! " Irais called out as we passed ; " you'll be indeed a cold fowl if you stand there motionless, and every one prefers them hot in weather like this ! "

And then we all laughed exceedingly, as though the most splendid joke had been made, and before we had done we were out of the village and in the open country beyond, and could see my house and garden far away behind, glittering in the sunshine ; and in front of us lay the forest, with its vistas of pines stretching away into infinity, and a drive through it of fourteen miles before we reached the sea. It was a hoar-frost day, and the forest was an enchanted forest leading into fairyland, and though Irais and I have been there often before, and always thought it beautiful, yet yesterday we stood under the final arch of frosted trees, struck silent by the sheer loveliness of the place. For a long way out the sea was frozen, and then there was a deep blue line, and a cluster of motionless orange sails ; at our feet a narrow strip of pale yellow sand ; right and left the line of sparkling forest ; and we ourselves standing in a world of white and diamond traceries. The stillness of an eternal Sunday lay on the place like a benediction.

Minora broke the silence by remarking that Dresden was pretty, but she thought this beat it almost.

" I don't quite see," said Irais in a hushed voice, as though she were in a holy place, " how the two can be compared."

" Yes, Dresden is more convenient, of course," replied Minora ; after which we

turned away and thought we would keep her
quiet by feeding her, so we went back to the
sleigh and had the horses taken out and their
cloths put on, and they were walked up and
down a distant glade while we sat in the
sleigh and picnicked. It *is* a hard day for
the horses,—nearly thirty miles there and
back and no stable in the middle; but they
are so fat and spoiled that it cannot do
them much harm sometimes to taste the
bitterness of life. I warmed soup in a little
apparatus I have for such occasions, which
helped to take the chilliness off the sandwiches,—this is the only unpleasant part of
a winter picnic, the clammy quality of the
provisions just when you most long for
something very hot. Minora let her nose
very carefully out of its wrappings, took a
mouthful, and covered it up quickly again.
She was nervous lest it should be frost-
nipped, and truth compels me to add that
her nose is not a bad nose, and might even
be pretty on anybody else; but she does not
know how to carry it, and there is an art in
the angle at which one's nose is held just

as in everything else, and really noses were intended for something besides mere blowing.

It is the most difficult thing in the world to eat sandwiches with immense fur and woollen gloves on, and I think we ate almost as much fur as anything, and choked exceedingly during the process. Minora was angry at this, and at last pulled off her glove, but quickly put it on again.

" How very unpleasant," she remarked after swallowing a large piece of fur.

" It will wrap round your pipes, and keep them warm," said Irais.

" Pipes ! " echoed Minora, greatly disgusted by such vulgarity.

" I'm afraid I can't help you," I said, as she continued to choke and splutter ; " we are all in the same case, and I don't know how to alter it."

" There are such things as forks, I suppose," snapped Minora.

" That's true," said I, crushed by the obviousness of the remedy ; but of what use are forks if they are fifteen miles off ?

So Minora had to continue to eat her gloves.

By the time we had finished, the sun was already low behind the trees and the clouds beginning to flush a faint pink. The old coachman was given sandwiches and soup, and while he led the horses up and down with one hand and held his lunch in the other, we packed up—or, to be correct, I packed, and the others looked on and gave me valuable advice.

This coachman, Peter by name, is seventy years old, and was born on the place, and has driven its occupants for fifty years, and I am nearly as fond of him as I am of the sun-dial; indeed, I don't know what I should do without him, so entirely does he appear to understand and approve of my tastes and wishes. No drive is too long or difficult for the horses if I want to take it, no place impossible to reach if I want to go to it, no weather or roads too bad to prevent my going out if I wish to—to all my suggestions he responds with the readiest cheerfulness, and smoothes away all objections raised by the Man of Wrath, who rewards his alacrity in doing my pleasure by speaking of him as an *alter Esel*. In the summer, on fine evenings, I love to drive late and alone in the scented forests, ànd when I have reached a dark part stop, and sit quite still, listening to the nightingales repeating their little tune over and over again after interludes of gurgling, or if there are no nightingales, listening to the marvellous silence, and letting its blessedness descend into my very soul. The nightingales in the forests about here all sing the same tune, and in the same key (E flat)

. I don't

know whether all nightingales do this, or if it is peculiar to this particular spot. When they have sung it once, they clear their throats a little, and hesitate, and then do it again, and it is the prettiest little song in the world. How could I indulge my passion for these drives with their pauses without Peter ? He is so used to them that he stops now at the right moment without having to

be told, and he is ready to drive me all
night if I wish it, with no sign of anything
but cheerful willingness on his nice old face.
The Man of Wrath deplores these eccentric
tastes, as he calls them, of mine ; but has
given up trying to prevent my indulging
them because, while he is deploring in one
part of the house, I have slipped out at a
door in the other, and am gone before he can
catch me, and have reached and am lost in
the shadows of the forest by the time he has
discovered that I am nowhere to be found.

The brightness of Peter's perfections are
sullied however by one spot, and that is,
that as age creeps upon him, he not only
cannot hold the horses in if they don't want
to be held in, but he goes to sleep sometimes
on his box if I have him out too soon after
lunch, and has upset me twice within the
last year—once last winter out of a sleigh,
and once this summer, when the horses shied
at a bicycle, and bolted into the ditch on
one side of the *chaussee* (German for high
road), and the bicycle was so terrified at the
horses shying that it shied too into the ditch

on the other side, and the carriage was
smashed, and the bicycle was smashed, and
we were all very unhappy, except Peter, who
never lost his pleasant smile, and looked
so placid that my tongue clave to the roof
of my mouth when I tried to make it scold
him.

" But I should think he ought to have
been *thoroughly* scolded on an occasion like
that," said Minora, to whom I had been
telling this story as we wandered on the
yellow sands while the horses were being
put in the sleigh; and she glanced nervously
up at Peter, whose mild head was visible
between the bushes above us. " Shall we
get home before dark ? " she asked.

The sun had altogether disappeared behind
the pines and only the very highest of the
little clouds were still pink ; out at sea the
mists were creeping up, and the sails of
the fishing-smacks had turned a dull brown;
a flight of wild geese passed across the disc
of the moon with loud cacklings.

" Before dark ? " echoed Irais, " I should
think not. It is dark now nearly in the

forest, and we shall have the loveliest moonlight drive back."

" But it is surely very dangerous to let a man who goes to sleep drive you," said Minora apprehensively.

" But he's such an old dear," I said.

" Yes, yes, no doubt," she replied testily ; " but there are wakeful old dears to be had, and on a box they are preferable."

Irais laughed. " You are growing quite amusing, Miss Minora," she said.

" He isn't on a box to-day," said I ; " and I never knew him go to sleep standing up behind us on a sleigh."

But Minora was not to be appeased, and muttered something about seeing no fun in foolhardiness, which shows how alarmed she was, for it was rude.

Peter, however, behaved beautifully on the way home, and Irais and I at least were as happy as possible driving back, with all the glories of the western sky flashing at us every now and then at the end of a long avenue as we swiftly passed, and later on, when they had faded, myriads of stars in the narrow black strip of sky over our heads. It was bitterly cold, and Minora was silent, and not in the least inclined to laugh with us as she had been six hours before.

"Have you enjoyed yourself, Miss Minora ? " inquired Irais, as we got out of the forest on to the *chaussee*, and the lights of the village before ours twinkled in the distance.

"How many degrees do you suppose there are now ? " was Minora's reply to this question.

"Degrees ?—Of frost ? Oh, dear me, are you cold ? " cried Irais solicitously.

"Well, it isn't exactly warm, is it ? " said Minora sulkily ; and Irais pinched me. "Well, but think how much colder you would have been without all that fur you ate for lunch inside you," she said.

"And what a nice chapter you will be able to write about the Baltic," said I. "Why, it is practically certain that you are the first English person who has ever been to just this part of it."

"Isn't there some English poem," said

Irais, "about being the first who ever burst——"

" ' Into that silent sea,' " finished Minora hastily. " You can't quote that without its context, you know."

" But I wasn't going to," said Irais meekly, " I only paused to breathe. I must breathe, or perhaps I might die."

The lights from my energetic friend's *Schloss* shone brightly down upon us as we passed round the base of the hill on which it stands ; she is very proud of this hill, as well she may be, seeing that it is the only one in the whole district.

" Do you never go there ? " asked Minora, jerking her head in the direction of the house.

" Sometimes. She is a very busy woman, and I should feel I was in the way if I went often."

" It would be interesting to see another North German interior," said Minora ; " and I should be obliged if you would take me."

" But I can't fall upon her suddenly with a strange girl," I protested ; " and we are not at all on such intimate terms as to justify my taking all my visitors to see her."

"What do you want to see another interior for ? " asked Irais. "I can tell you what it is like ; and if you went nobody would speak to you, and if you were to ask questions, and began to take notes, the good lady would stare at you in the frankest amazement, and think Elizabeth had brought a young lunatic out for an airing. *Everybody* is not as patient as Elizabeth," added Irais, anxious to pay off old scores.

"I would do a great deal for you, Miss Minora," I said, " but I can't do that."

"If we went," said Irais, " Elizabeth and I would be placed with great ceremony on a sofa behind a large, polished oval table with a crochet-mat in the centre — it *has* got a crochet-mat in the centre, hasn't it ? " I nodded. "And you would sit on one of the four little podgy, buttony, tasselly red chairs that are ranged on the other side of the table facing the sofa. They *are* red, Elizabeth ? " Again I nodded. "The floor

is painted yellow, and there is no carpet
except a rug in front of the sofa.   The paper
is dark chocolate colour, almost black ; that
is in order that after years of use the dirt
may not show, and the room need not be
done up.   Dirt is like wickedness, you see,
Miss Minora—its being there never matters;
it is only when it shows so much as to be
apparent to everybody that we are ashamed
of it.   At intervals round the high walls are
chairs, and cabinets with lamps on them,
and in one corner is a great white cold stove
—or is it majolica ? " she asked, turning
to me.

" No, it is white."

" There are a great many lovely big
windows, all ready to let in the air and the
sun, but they are as carefully covered with
brown lace curtains under heavy stuff ones
as though a whole row of houses were just
opposite, with peering eyes at every window
trying to look in, instead of there only being
fields, and trees, and birds. No fire, no
sunlight, no books, no flowers ; but a
consoling smell of red cabbage coming up

under the door, mixed, in due season, with soapsuds."

" When did you go there ? " asked Minora.

" Ah, when did I go there indeed ?   When did I not go there ?   I have been calling there all my life."

Minora's eyes rolled doubtfully first at me then at Irais from the depths of her head-wrappings ; they are large eyes with long dark eyelashes, and far be it from me to deny that each eye taken by itself is fine, but they are put in all wrong.

" The only thing you would learn there," went on Irais, " would be the significance of sofa corners in Germany.   If we three went there together, I should be ushered into the right-hand corner of the sofa, because it is the place of honour, and I am the greatest stranger ; Elizabeth would be invited to seat herself in the left-hand corner, as next in importance ; the hostess would sit near us in an arm-chair ; and you, as a person of no importance whatever, would either be left to sit where you could, or would be put

on a chair facing us, and with the entire
breadth of the table between us to mark
the immense social gulf that separates the
married woman from the mere virgin. These
sofa corners make the drawing of nice dis-
tinctions possible in a way that nothing
else could. The world might come to an
end, and create less sensation in doing it,
than you would, Miss Minora, if by any
chance you got into the right-hand corner
of one. That you are put on a chair on
the other side of the table places you at once
in the scale of precedence, and exactly defines
your social position, or rather your complete
want of a social position." And Irais tilted
her nose ever so little heavenwards. " Note
it," she added, " as the heading of your next
chapter."

" Note what ? " asked Minora impatiently.

" Why, ' The Subtle Significance of Sofas '
of course," replied Irais. " If," she continued, as Minora made no reply appreciative
of this suggestion, " you were to call unexpectedly, the bad luck which pursues the
innocent would most likely make you hit

on a washing-day, and the distracted mistress of the house would keep you waiting in the cold room so long while she changed her dress, that you would begin to fear you were to be left to perish from want and hunger ; and when she did appear, would show by the bitterness of her welcoming smile the rage that was boiling in her heart."

" But what has the mistress of the house to do with washing ? "

" What has she to do with washing ? Oh, you sweet innocent—pardon my familiarity, but such ignorance of country-life customs is very touching in one who is writing a book about them."

" Oh, I have no doubt I am very ignorant," said Minora loftily.

" Seasons of washing," explained Irais, " are seasons set apart by the *Hausfrau* to be kept holy. They only occur every two or three months, and while they are going on the whole house is in an uproar, every other consideration sacrificed, husband and children sunk into insignificance, and no one approaching, or interfering with, the mistress of the house during these days of purification, but at their peril."

" You don't really mean," said Minora, " that you only wash your clothes four times a year ? "

" Yes, I do mean it," replied Irais.

" Well, I think that is very disgusting," said Minora emphatically.

Irais raised those pretty, delicate eyebrows of hers. " Then you must take care and not marry a German," she said.

" But what is the object of it ? " went on Minora.

" Why, to clean the linen, I suppose."

" Yes, yes, but why only at such long intervals ? "

" It is an outward and visible sign of vast possessions in the shape of linen. If you were to want to have your clothes washed every week, as you do in England, you would be put down as a person who only has just enough to last that length of time, and would be an object of general contempt."

" But I should be a clean object," cried

Minora, " and my house would not be full
of accumulated dirt."

We said nothing—there was nothing to be
said.

" It must be a happy land, that England
of yours," Irais remarked after a while with
a sigh—a beatific vision no doubt presenting
itself to her mind of a land full of washer-
women, and agile gentlemen darting at
door-handles.

" It is a *clean* land, at any rate," replied
Minora.

" *I* don't want to go and live in it," I
said—for we were driving up to the house,
and a memory of fogs and umbrellas came
into my mind as I looked up fondly at its
dear old west front, and I felt that what I
want is to live and die just here, and that
there never was such a happy woman as
Elizabeth.

April 18*th*.—I have been so busy ever
since Irais and Minora left that I can hardly
believe the spring is here, and the garden
hurrying on its green and flowered petticoat

—only its petticoat as yet, for though the underwood is a fairy-land of tender little leaves, the trees above are still quite bare.

February was gone before I well knew that it had come, so deeply was I engaged in making hot-beds, and having them sown with petunias, verbenas, and nicotina affinis; while no less than thirty are dedicated solely to vegetables, it having been borne in upon me lately that vegetables must be interesting things to grow, besides possessing solid virtues not given to flowers, and that I might as well take the orchard and kitchen garden under my wing. So I have rushed in with all the zeal of utter inexperience, and my February evenings were spent poring over gardening books, and my days in applying the freshly absorbed wisdom. Who says that February is a dull, sad, slow month in the country ? It was of the cheerfullest, swiftest description here, and its mild days enabled me to get on beautifully with the digging and manuring, and filled my rooms with snowdrops. The longer I live the greater is my respect and affection for manure in all its forms, and already, though the year is so young, a considerable portion of its pin-money has been spent on artificial manure. The Man of Wrath says he never met a young woman who spent her money that way before; I remarked that it must be nice to have an original wife; and he retorted that the word original hardly described me, and that the word eccentric was the one required. Very well, I suppose I am eccentric, since even my husband says so; but if my eccentricities are of such a practical nature as to result later in the biggest cauliflowers and tenderest lettuce in Prussia, why then he ought to be the first to rise up and call me blessèd.

I sent to England for vegetable-marrow seeds, as they are not grown here, and people try and make boiled cucumbers take their place; but boiled cucumbers are nasty things, and I don't see why marrows should not do here perfectly well. These, and primrose-roots, are the English contributions to my garden. I brought over the roots in a tin box last time I came from

England, and am anxious to see whether
they will consent to live here. Certain it is
that they don't exist in the Fatherland, so
I can only conclude the winter kills them,
for surely, if such lovely things would grow,
they never would have been overlooked.
Irais is deeply interested in the experiment;
she reads so many English books, and has
heard so much about primroses, and they
have got so mixed up in her mind with
leagues, and dames, and Disraelis, that she
longs to see this mysterious political flower,
and has made me promise to telegraph
when it appears, and she will come over.
But they are not going to do anything this
year, and I only hope those cold days did
not send them off to the Paradise of flowers.
I am afraid their first impression of Germany
was a chilly one.

Irais writes about once a week, and in-
quires after the garden and the babies, and
announces her intention of coming back as
soon as the numerous relations staying with
her have left,—" which they won't do," she
wrote the other day, " until the first frosts

nip them off, when they will disappear like belated dahlias—double ones of course, for single dahlias are too charming to be compared to relations. I have every sort of cousin and uncle and aunt here, and here they have been ever since my husband's birthday—not the same ones exactly, but I get so confused that I never know where one ends and the other begins. My husband goes off after breakfast to look at his crops, he says, and I am left at their mercy. I wish I had crops to go and look at—I should be grateful even for one, and would look at it from morning till night, and quite stare it out of countenance, sooner than stay at home and have the truth told me by enigmatic aunts. Do you know my Aunt Bertha? She, in particular, spends her time propounding obscure questions for my solution. I get so tired and worried trying to guess the answers, which are always truths supposed to be good for me to hear. ' Why do you wear your hair on your forehead ? ' she asks, — and that sets me off wondering why I *do* wear it on my forehead, and what she wants to know for, or whether she does know and only wants to know if I will answer truthfully. 'I am sure I don't know, aunt,' I say meekly, after puzzling over it for ever so long ; 'perhaps my maid knows. Shall I ring and ask her ? ' And then she informs me that I wear it so to hide an ugly line she says I have down the middle of my forehead, and that betokens a listless and discontented disposition. Well, if she knew, what did she ask me for ? Whenever I am with them they ask me riddles like that, and I simply lead a *dog's* life. Oh, my dear, relations are like drugs,—useful, sometimes, and even pleasant, if taken in small quantities and seldom, but dreadfully pernicious on the whole, and the truly wise avoid them."

From Minora I have only had one communication since her departure, in which she thanked me for her pleasant visit, and said she was sending me a bottle of English embrocation to rub on my bruises after skating ; that it was wonderful stuff, and she was sure I would like it ; and that it cost two marks, and would I send stamps. I pondered long over this. Was it a parting hit, intended as revenge for our having laughed at her? Was she personally interested in the sale of embrocation? Or was it merely Minora's idea of a graceful return for my hospitality? As for bruises, nobody who skates decently regards it as a bruise-producing exercise, and whenever there were any they were all on Minora; but she did happen to turn round once, I remember, just as I was in the act of tumbling down for the first and only time, and her delight was but thinly veiled by her excessive solicitude and sympathy. I sent her the stamps, received the bottle, and resolved to let her drop out of my life; I had been a good Samaritan to her at the request of my friend, but the best of Samaritans resents the offer of healing oil for his own use.

But why waste a thought on Minora at Easter, the real beginning of the year in defiance of calendars? She belongs to the winter that is past, to the darkness that is over, and has no part or lot in the life I shall lead for the next six months. Oh, I could dance and sing for joy that the spring is here! What a resurrection of beauty there is in my garden, and of brightest hope in my heart! The whole of this radiant Easter day I have spent out of doors, sitting at first among the windflowers and celandines, and then, later, walking with the babies to the Hirschwald, to see what the spring had been doing there ; and the afternoon was so hot that we lay a long time on the turf, blinking up through the leafless branches of the silver birches at the soft, fat little white clouds floating motionless in the blue. We had tea on the grass in the sun, and when it began to grow late, and the babies were in bed, and all the little windflowers folded up for the night, I still wandered in the green paths, my heart full of happiest gratitude. It makes one very humble to see oneself surrounded by such a wealth of beauty and perfection *anonymously* lavished, and to think of the infinite meanness of our own grudging charities. and how displeased we are if they are not promptly and properly appreciated. I do sincerely trust that the benediction that is always awaiting me in my garden may by degrees be more deserved, and that I may grow in grace, and patience, and cheerfulness, just like the happy flowers I so much love.

THE END

Also of interest

ELIZABETH VON ARNIM
Vera
Fraülein Schmidt and
 Mr Anstruther

DOROTHY RICHARDSON
Pilgrimage (4 vols)

ELIOT BLISS
Luminous Isle

E H YOUNG
Miss Mole
The Misses Mallett

MARGARET KENNEDY
The Ladies of Lyndon
Together and Apart
The Constant Nymph

SARAH GRAND
The Beth Book

ROSAMOND LEHMANN
The Ballad and the Source
The Gipsy's Baby
Invitation to the Waltz
A Note in Music
A Sea-Grape Tree
The Weather in the Streets

RADCLYFFE HALL
The Unlit Lamp
The Well of Loneliness

STORM JAMESON
Love in Winter
None Turn Back

SYLVIA TOWNSEND WARNER
Mr Fortune's Maggot
The True Heart

REBECCA WEST
The Fountain Overflows
The Thinking Reed
Harriet Hume
The Harsh Voice
The Judge
The Return of the Soldier

MAY SINCLAIR
Life and Death of Harriett Frean
Mary Olivier: A Life
The Three Sisters

E ARNOT ROBERTSON
Ordinary Families
Four Frightened People

F M MAYOR
The Third Miss Symons

ROSE MACAULAY
Told by an Idiot
The World my Wilderness

ELIZABETH JENKINS
The Tortoise and the Hare

F TENNYSON JESSE
The Lacquer Lady
A Pin to see the Peepshow

VIRAGO MODERN CLASSICS

The first Virago Modern Classic, *Frost in May* by Antonia White, was published in 1978. It launched a list dedicated to the celebration of women writers and to the rediscovery and reprinting of their works. Its aim was, and is, to demonstrate the existence of a female tradition in fiction which is both enriching and enjoyable. The Leavisite notion of the 'Great Tradition', and the narrow, academic definition of a 'classic', has meant the neglect of a large number of interesting secondary works of fiction. In calling the series 'Modern Classics' we do not necessarily mean 'great' — although this is often the case. Published with new critical and biographical introductions, books are chosen for many reasons: sometimes for their importance in literary history; sometimes because they illuminate particular aspects of womens' lives, both personal and public. They may be classics of comedy or storytelling; their interest can be historical, feminist, political or literary.

Initially the Virago Modern Classics concentrated on English novels and short stories published in the early decades of this century. As the series has grown it has broadened to include works of fiction from different centuries, different countries, cultures and literary traditions. In 1984 the Victorian Classics were launched; there are separate lists of Irish, Scottish, European, American, Australian and other English speaking countries; there are books written by Black women, by Catholic and Jewish women, and a few relevant novels by men. There is, too, a companion series of Non-Fiction Classics constituting biography, autobiography, travel, journalism, essays, poetry, letters and diaries.

By the end of 1986 over 250 titles will have been published in these two series, many of which have been suggested by our readers.